Chip Hilton Sports Series

#5

A Pass and A Prayer

Coach Clair Bee

Updated by Randall and Cynthia Bee Farley

Foreword by Bob Knight

**BROADMAN
& HOLMAN
PUBLISHERS**

Nashville, Tennessee

0-8054-1987-X

Published by Broadman & Holman Publishers,
Nashville, Tennessee
Page Design: Anderson Thomas Design, Nashville, Tennessee
Typesetting: PerfecType, Nashville, Tennessee

Subject Heading: FOOTBALL—FICTION / YOUTH
Library of Congress Card Catalog Number: 98-50759

Library of Congress Cataloging-in-Publication Data
Bee, Clair.
    A pass and a prayer / by Clair Bee ; [edited by Cynthia
Bee Farley, Randall K. Farley].
        p.   cm. — (Chip Hilton sports series ; v. 5)
    Updated ed. of a work published in 1951.
    Summary: The final season of team captain Chip's foot-
ball career at Valley Falls High finds him fighting a new
coach, who threatens to destroy the fair play, sportsmanship,
and good citizenship that have made his team great.
    ISBN 0-8054-1987-X (pbk.)
    [1. Football—Fiction. 2. Sportsmanship—Fiction.]
I. Farley, Cynthia Bee, 1952–   . II. Farley, Randall K.,
1952–   . III. Title. IV. Series: Bee, Clair. Chip Hilton sports
series ; v. 5.

PZ7.B38196Pas   1999
[Fic]—dc21   98-50759
                                                    CIP
                                                    AC

1 2 3 4 5 03 02 01 00 99

The Chip Hilton Sports Series

For more information on
Chip Hilton-related activities and to correspond
with other Chip fans, check the Internet at
chiphilton.com

TO OUR PARENTS

WILLIAM and DORIS HELMONDOLLAR
(Pappaw and Nana)
and
CLAIR and MARY BEE
(Pop-Pop and Mum-Mum)

Our Hank Rockwells and Mary Hiltons.
They taught us teamwork begins with
two or more working as one.

LOVE,
RANDY AND CINDY
MAY 1998

Contents

CONTENTS

Foreword

THERE IS nothing that could be a greater honor for me than to be able to write the foreword to the new editions of the Chip Hilton books written by Clair Bee and revised by his daughter Cindy and son-in-law Randy.

I can remember that in the early and midfifties, when I was in junior high and high school, there was nothing more exciting, outside of actually playing a game, than reading one of the books from Coach Bee's Chip Hilton series. He wrote twenty-three books in all, and I bought and read each one of them during my student days. His books were about the three sports that I played—football, basketball, and baseball—and had the kind of characters in them that every young boy wanted to imagine that he was or could become.

Chip Hilton himself was a combination of everything that was good, right, and fair in athletic competition. His accomplishments on the field, on the floor, or on the diamond were the things that made every boy's dreams.

Henry Rockwell was the kind of coach that every boy wanted to play for, and he knew how to get the best out of every boy who played for him.

My mother and grandmother used to take me shopping with them in Akron and would leave me at the bookstore in O'Neil's department store with $1.25 to purchase the Chip Hilton book of my choice. It would invariably take me at least two hours to decide which of these wonderfully vivid episodes in athletic competition, struggle, and accomplishment I would purchase.

As I read my way through the entire series, I learned there was a much greater value to what Clair Bee had written than just the lifelike portrayal of athletic competition. His books had a tremendous sense of right and wrong, what was fair and what wasn't, and what the word *sportsmanship* was all about.

During the first year I was at the United States Military Academy at West Point as an assistant basketball coach, I had the opportunity to meet Clair Bee, the author of those great stories that were such an integral part of my boyhood dreams. After all, no boy could have ever read those wonderful stories without imagining himself as Chip Hilton.

Clair Bee became one of the two most influential people in my career as a college coach. I have never met a man whose intelligence I have admired more. No one person has ever contributed more to the game of basketball in the development of the fundamental skills, tactics, and strategies of the game than Clair Bee during his fifty years as a teacher of the sport. I strongly believe that the same can be said of his authorship of the Chip Hilton series.

It seems that every day I am asked by a parent, "What can be done to interest my son in sports?" Or "What is the best thing I can do for my son, who really has shown an interest in sports?" For the past thirty-three years, when I have been asked those questions, I have always answered by saying, "Have your son read about Chip Hilton." Then I've explained a little bit about the Chip Hilton series.

The enjoyment that a young athlete can get from reading the Chip Hilton series is just as great today as it was for me more than forty years ago. The lessons that Clair Bee teaches through Chip Hilton and his exploits are the most meaningful and priceless examples of what is right and fair about life that I have ever read. I have the entire series in a glass case in my library at home. I still spend a lot of hours browsing through those twenty-three books.

As a coach, I will always be indebted to Clair Bee for the many hours he spent helping me learn about the game of basketball. As a person, I owe an even greater debt to him for providing me with the most memorable reading of my youth through his series on Chip Hilton.

BOB KNIGHT
Head Coach, Men's Basketball, Indiana University

CHAPTER 1

The New Coach Makes a Hit

WILLIAM "CHIP" HILTON, Valley Falls High School's all-state quarterback, dug his cleats in short, driving steps toward the football resting on the tee and drove the toe of his kicking shoe squarely against the dirt mark he had placed on the ball a few seconds earlier. The tremendous power in the lanky athlete's vicious forward thrust exploded through the ball, and before the spectators in the stands heard the thud of shoe against pigskin, the ball arched swiftly out and up, end over end for Midwestern's goal line. A continuous roar erupted from the stands as the blue- and red-uniformed figures burst into action.

The tall kicker followed the ball's downfield flight with long strides that ate up the distance. He quickly edged yards ahead of his teammates. Chip Hilton could really move, and he knew how to speed past would-be blockers as if they weren't even there. With a joyous grunt of exultation, Hilton met the Prep ball carrier head-on at the twenty-yard line, and again, before they heard the crash of the two bodies, the fans saw the ball shoot out along the ground amid a wild scramble, which ended when the tackler's red-clad arms pulled the ball close to his body and his legs curled protectively around the prize. So, less than ten seconds after the scrimmage between Valley Falls High School and Midwestern Preparatory School had begun, the Big Reds had recovered the kickoff and the ball was on the Prep twenty-two-yard line, first down and ten to go.

Hilton was up and back behind the ball, waiting for his teammates to join him before half of them reached the huddle. "C'mon, guys!" he cried. "Let's go!"

The Big Reds needed no urging. While Midwestern was trying to get organized, Speed Morris, Valley Falls's elusive ball carrier, slashed inside the right tackle for six, Chris Badger hit the center for two, and Cody Collins drove to the eight-yard line on a cross buck for the first down. Before the linesmen could move the chain, the Big Reds were out of the huddle, into their T-formation, and Hilton was calling the signals.

"31-48-22!"

A mass of bodies merged, forming a pileup in the center of the line, and then Hilton leaped into the air, rifling a bullet pass to his left end just at the goal line for a touchdown. Seconds later, the blond quarterback booted the extra point and trotted back up the field. He felt good.

The Prep students had eagerly thronged to the stadium to see Midwestern slaughter Valley Falls. Now they were stunned.

"This isn't supposed to happen! *Seven* points in less than a minute! Seven points!"

"Who's that guy? That 44?"

"That's Hilton! All-state! Best quarterback in the country!"

"You can say that again! Kicks off, makes the tackle, recovers the fumble, and passes for a touchdown!"

"*And kicks* the extra point! What a player!"

"The whole team's like that!"

"They must have been practicin' a month!"

The last statement was an exaggeration. The Big Reds of Valley Falls had been practicing only four days. Coach Henry "Rock" Rockwell was fortunate to have his championship team intact from the previous year with the exception of one end and a guard. The squad knew Rockwell's T-formation plays by heart. More than that, every veteran had reported in top condition.

At that very moment, the veteran mentor was executing a slow-motion block for two reserves near the bench. Rockwell believed in keeping himself and all the Big Reds on their toes every possible second.

The other members of the coaching staff were busy too. Chet Stewart, one of Rock's former players and now his first assistant, was working with the reserve line. Tom Brasher, new to Valley Falls High School, was putting the novices through signals in front of the bleachers, where most of the Prep students were sitting. Brasher had been with the Big Reds only four days.

Under the goal, where the last bit of action had taken place, Bill Richards, the new Midwestern coach, was surrounded by the entire Prep squad. He was irate. The Big Reds regulars, grouped near the center of the field, couldn't hear what Richards was saying, but they could see his arms waving.

"Things will be different now," Biggie Cohen drawled, nodding toward the Prep team. "The party is over!"

Soapy Smith whistled ominously and, after a cautious glance toward the bench to make sure Rockwell wasn't watching, began limping around on the inside of the little circle. "Oh, my ankle," he moaned, "my poor ankle! Wonder why the Rockhead doesn't take me out? He knows I carry this team on my back!"

Red Schwartz snorted. "Hah! The only thing you carry on your back is number 88 and the Gatorade for the players!"

Soapy ignored Red and continued his limp, moaning and grumbling. "Bet the little Prepsidoodles are gonna be real mad now!"

"Looks like someone else is real mad," Speed Morris said softly, pointing cautiously toward the sidelines.

Tom Brasher, the new member of the Valley Falls coaching staff, wasn't a bit angry, but no one could tell that by his actions. He looked as if he was on a rampage, stamping back and forth in front of Josh Connors, Hilton's understudy, waving his arms, and bellowing at the unfortunate youngster who had apparently made some kind of mistake. It was a good act, but it had no effect upon the regulars out on the field.

"Seems to be excited about something," Red Schwartz remarked dryly.

"Maybe he studied electrocution," Soapy quipped.

Schwartz shook his head. "No, Soapy," he said soothingly, "you mean elocution. We *got* to get him that thesaurus, guys!"

"What's the difference?" Soapy asked aggressively. "Electrocution, elocution, execution—hah! Depends on how they're used! Besides—"

"Look!" Morris interrupted. "What's all *that* about?"

The new coach had crouched in the defensive right-end position while the skeleton team was coming up to the ball in the T-formation. Connors was in the quarterback spot, his voice ringing out clearly and with much the same vibrant decisiveness Hilton employed.

With the snap of the ball, Connors turned left, pivoted, and followed his interference toward his right end on an in-and-out sweep. Brasher charged across the line at the same time and sprinted after Josh, catching up with the young quarterback and dropping him to the ground with a vicious tackle from the rear. The contact was so sudden and the weight of the tackler so overpowering that the little ball carrier doubled back over Brasher's shoulder. Then the driving momentum of the tackle lifted the boy and smashed him brutally to the ground.

"What's he trying to do?" Cohen cried.

Brasher scrambled to his feet and trotted back to the defensive end position, glancing quickly at the bleachers to make sure the spectators appreciated his performance. But he was disappointed. The Prep fans had quieted suddenly. They were anxiously looking at the little quarterback bravely trying to get to his feet. But Connors couldn't make it, and he fell back on the ground writhing in pain.

Chip Hilton's reaction was automatic. Without thinking, he dashed off the field and over to Connors's side. Biggie Cohen followed. Josh was again struggling to stand. "Stay down, Josh," Chip said softly. "Let Pop take a look at your leg."

"I'm all right, Chip," Josh insisted, trying to push himself upright. "I just didn't know he was going to tackle me."

Brasher came back just in time to hear the words. "Didn't know I was gonna tackle you!" he grated. "What did you think I was gonna do, kiss you?"

"Sorry, Coach," Josh tried to explain, "but we were running signals, and I just didn't expect anyone to tackle me."

"Well, expect it the next time," Brasher interrupted harshly, "and keep in mind that football's a game of speed. When you're carryin' the goods, you gotta move! If you don't move, you get tackled! Now, come on, get up on your feet. And *this* time, *move* when you carry the ball!"

But Connors was in no shape to move; he could hardly stand. So Chip and Biggie half-led, half-carried him to the bench where Pop Brown, the Big Reds trainer, took over. Chip and Biggie stood next to Pop for a second, worried about Josh's leg and disturbed by a growing resentment toward Tom Brasher. The Big Reds weren't used to that kind of coaching.

Rockwell's voice jarred the two players into action. "Let's go, Chip! Biggie! Step on it!"

Chip and Biggie swung around, surprised to find Midwestern lined up to receive and their teammates spread across the field behind the ball. They hurried toward their positions but, on the way, each glanced swiftly at Brasher. The new assistant coach was standing right where they'd left him, hands on hips, glaring in their direction.

"How come the Rock lets him get away with that stuff?" Biggie demanded angrily.

"He didn't see it, Biggie," Chip explained quietly. Cohen grunted with disgust.

"Well, he shoulda seen it!" he growled. "Lots of things he shoulda seen about that guy the last couple of days! If he starts any of that with me—"

Biggie didn't finish the sentence, but Chip knew exactly what he meant. Chip adjusted the ball on the tee and dropped back to his normal starting position, thinking the same thing. This wasn't the first time Brasher had smashed into an unsuspecting scrub in the past three days. Most of the reserves were willing but inexperienced, and not one of them carried enough weight to absorb the crushing jar of Brasher's solid 220 pounds. Chip couldn't help wishing the new coach would try a couple of his demonstrations on Biggie. He glanced at his friend's powerful back and grinned. The Rock had said Biggie was the strongest athlete he'd ever known. And the Rock had known a lot of them.

The referee's whistle shrilled, and Chip concentrated on a spot on the ball. He met it solidly, sending the kick high enough to give his teammates time to get well down the field. He knew from the feel of the impact that the ball would reach the goal line. Chip tore straight down the middle of the field toward the receiver, and once again he made the tackle. But the ball carrier didn't fumble this time; he wrapped both arms around the ball and squeezed it hard into his stomach.

Bill Richards, Midwestern's coach, didn't use the huddle. So the Prepsters lined up in regular T-formation first, ran or passed from it, or shifted to a single wing. But no matter what formation or play they used, the Big Reds stopped them cold.

Most quarterbacks like to test their opponents with an off-tackle slant, and the Prep field general was no exception. He ran his first scrimmage play right at Biggie Cohen, the Big Reds left tackle. That was a bad call. Cohen was the biggest player on the field, packing 220 pounds on his six-four frame. Midwestern's star running back stopped as if he had run into a force field. He took a long time getting up, even with Biggie's helping hand. A thrust into the line was smeared as efficiently by Lou Mazotta, the Big Reds quiet, serious-faced tackle known as "Mr. Four-by-Four."

A PASS AND A PRAYER

The desperate quarterback gambled on a long, down-the-middle pass but lost. Chip had shifted the Big Reds defense into a five-three-two-one on third down and ten, with Nick Trullo, Soapy Smith, and Chris Badger backing up the line, Speed Morris and Cody Collins on the wings, and himself in the safety position.

The long toss was meant for the converging ends, but Chip kept behind them until the ball nosed downward. Then he flashed forward, leaped high in the air, and gathered in the spinning ball. It almost seemed as if the Big Reds had planned the interception, judging by the way they sprang up ahead of their racing captain and mowed down the frantic opponents. Chip crossed the goal line standing up.

Once again the stands buzzed. Midwestern fans were bewildered. The sudden sprint and the second tally came almost as unexpectedly and explosively as the first score had.

"This *isn't* supposed to be happening!"

"Ditto! We been practicin' two weeks! This is supposed to be *our* year! Those guys can't be that good!"

"That quarterback's that good! That Hilton!"

"He ought to be! He's been all-state for a couple of years."

"The whole team's back! All but a couple of linemen!"

"You never know what they're gonna do!"

"You mean you don't know what *that* quarterback's gonna do!"

"You haven't seen anything yet! Wait until Hilton uses their spread formation and starts throwing strikes to his receivers!"

"What's the name of the coach? The old guy?"

"That's Rockwell! They call him the Rock! He's won more championships than any high school coach in the country! He's been coaching thirty-six years."

THE NEW COACH MAKES A HIT

"Thirty-six years? Must be seventy years old!"

Rockwell wasn't that old, but right at that moment he felt a lot older. All week he had been fighting a cold, fighting to stay on the job. This afternoon he had a fever, felt hot one minute, was shivering the next. He was also worried about the new assistant on his coaching staff. It wouldn't have been so bad if he had known something about Tom Brasher, something about his background and training.

Bill Thomas's sudden decision to move into the business world had caught Rockwell unaware, and before he could find a good replacement, Principal Zimmerman had told him that Mayor Condon and the school board had hired Brasher.

He discovered that Brasher was a close friend of Jerry Davis, an avowed enemy, but Rockwell had hoped for the best and welcomed the new coach with an open mind. But something about the man didn't seem quite right, and the veteran coach had sensed trouble. After four days of working together and cautious observation, Rockwell was sure he had identified his new assistant correctly. Tom Brasher was a know-it-all, a showoff, and a braggart.

The Big Reds' spirited play was the one thing that kept Rockwell going this afternoon. He shook off his cold, fever, and personal feelings, and forced himself to concentrate on his team.

After Chip converted the extra point following the second touchdown, Rockwell called for a time-out and sent Chip and his three backfield mates trotting to the sidelines.

"Tell Coach Brasher to send in the reserve backs, Chip," he said quietly. "You fellows better run through your signals. The timing wasn't too good on the cross buck!"

Soapy Smith waited until Rockwell was out of hearing, then protested. "That guy," he said deliberately, "wouldn't be satisfied if we scored a touchdown every play!" He snorted again. "Timing! Hah! Maybe each one of us oughta wear a stopwatch!" Jordan Taylor, Bill Carroll, Dan Harding, and Bob Blaine had just run onto the field when Brasher turned on Rockwell's first-string backfield.

"Now let's see if *you* fellows have any speed," he sneered, his penetrating black eyes focused full on Chip's face. "Let's see *you* go around right end on an in-and-out sweep, Hilton."

Chip took his place behind the center and checked the positions of his backs. But he had caught the hard glint in Brasher's menacing glance and, before starting the signals, noted that the new backfield coach had again assumed the defensive right-end position.

"19-64-77-41!"

On "41," Spike Davis snapped the ball into Chip's hands. Chip pivoted sharply, drove back three steps, and then picked up his interference. There was no indecision in the footwork of this backfield; the timing was precise. Brasher knew the starting signal and cheated a little in his desperate desire to overtake his next target. He sliced as close behind the line as possible and dove headlong at the back of Chip's legs. But just as Brasher's feet left the ground, Chip turned on a burst of speed and raced away behind the wall of interference. Brasher shot forward in a full belly flop and sprawled awkwardly on the ground.

Laughter rolled from the stands, and the chagrined coach scrambled to his feet, blazing with anger. But he couldn't do anything, not even when he saw Chip's backfield mates smiling and exchanging glances as they came trotting back. He could only glare with hate-filled eyes when Chip innocently asked, "Shall we run it again, Coach?"

There was a brief, awkward pause. When he realized Brasher was so angry he couldn't speak, Chip called the signals and began working with the backfield on the cross-buck timing. Chip had forgotten the whole incident, but Chip's teammates didn't forget it. They'd seen the evil look in Brasher's eyes as the disgruntled man watched the Big Reds captain and all-state quarterback. Every member of that veteran backfield knew Chip Hilton had incurred the burning enmity of Valley Falls's new backfield coach.

CHAPTER 2

Trouble for Rockwell

HENRY ROCKWELL had glanced toward the bleachers just as Brasher made his unsuccessful dive at Chip's flying legs; he'd heard the laughter from the stands, and he'd noted the furtive amusement of his star quarterback's running mates. All that the shrewd black eyes covered in that instant added up to what he'd feared: the kids who'd won the state championship the year before had figured Brasher correctly and had decided to cut him down to size.

Sick as he was, Rockwell couldn't resist a chuckle. The incident reflected Brasher's lack of intelligence and coaching ability. Chip Hilton was the fastest athlete in the state, and no one had ever been able to overtake him from behind. But the chuckle died almost as soon as it started. The Big Reds coach didn't like what he'd seen. For the past four days, Brasher had tried to impress the kids with his football knowledge and personal abilities. Rockwell had been disturbed by the reaction of the players. The little scene he'd just witnessed was the result, and there would be more incidents, probably more serious ones, unless Brasher could be curbed. Rockwell decided to have a talk with his new assistant the first thing in the morning.

On the field, the Midwestern team was making progress. The keen-eyed quarterback sensed the Valley Falls reserve backs were inexperienced and had taken advantage of the opportunity to fill the air with passes. They were clicking. Despite the furious charge of the Big Reds linemen, the Prep passer consistently found his receivers, flipping a short one over the line to an end, zipping a fast one to a back out in the flat, and then darting deep behind a wall of blockers to fire a long one over the middle. Prep's tall left end got behind Dan Harding on one of the distance flings, caught the spiraling ball without breaking stride, and raced across the goal line for the score.

On the sidelines, the Big Reds backfield regulars had paused in their signal practice to watch the action. As pass after pass clicked, they glanced anxiously in Rockwell's direction. These scrimmages with Midwestern were for keeps. For years the two schools had met in regularly scheduled games. But the competition had become too intense, had resulted in ill feeling, and the administrators of each school had decided against scheduling regular games. These informal scrimmages, therefore, provided the only opportunities for comparison of the merits of the two teams.

Midwestern was located in a small town a few miles from Valley Falls, and the Prep students were frequent evening and weekend visitors to the home town of the Big Reds. So it was not strange that faces and personalities were familiar to the players as well as to the fans.

A PASS AND A PRAYER

Henry Rockwell and Bill Richards knew exactly how the players on their teams felt about the scrimmage because they felt the same way. Both played to win, scrimmage or no scrimmage, but they didn't intend to let the workout get out of hand. After all, scrimmage scores never went into the record books. Their value was in checking the effectiveness of plays and particular defensive alignments and in the development of timing, blocking, and tackling under gamelike conditions. But both coaches took advantage of every opportunity to correct mistakes, and their frequent interruptions interfered with the smoothness of play.

The Big Reds coach was concentrating on his looping defense. Looping was one of Rockwell's favorite defenses, and its effectiveness depended upon the surprise shifting of the line one way and the backs in the opposite direction. The Big Reds were almost perfect in the maneuver; the players shifted in unison, left and right, right and left, on the voice signal as though pulled by a string. It was advantageous, too, for it completely demoralized the Preps' blocking assignments.

Effectiveness was never good enough for Rockwell. Every detail of execution had to be absolutely perfect to satisfy the Big Reds mentor. While he was concentrating on looping, the Prep quarterback was concentrating on his aerial success. Rockwell was so intensely absorbed with the line play that he hadn't even seemed to care that the Prepsters had scored four touchdowns through the air. But the members of the Rock's veteran backfield realized it, and they were aggravated almost as much as the Big Reds linemen who'd kept charging and charging, only to see the ball fly over their heads and land in the arms of a Prep receiver.

Chip and his backfield mates were so frustrated because of their enforced sideline inaction that they began to throw their bodies in imitation blocks toward imaginary Prep players every time they ran through a play. After Prep's fourth touchdown, however, Rockwell felt satisfied with the work of his forward wall, and he decided to give his ends and backs some attention. He called time and bellowed, "Let's go, Hilton. Bring that backfield over here. On the double now. Let's have a little life!"

Behind him, in the huddle, Soapy Smith mopped the sweat from his face with a perspiration-soaked sleeve and grunted. "Life," he hissed. "He should get a life! Slave driver! Now I suppose he'll make Chip throw passes for an hour, and I'll have to chase footballs all over the country!"

Biggie Cohen laughed. "All you have to do is catch 'em, freckle face. Start running with your hands up in the air, and when Chip drops the pill into 'em, squeeze! Get it? Squeeze! You don't have to chase 'em then."

The arrival of the varsity backs interrupted Soapy's retort, and Rockwell's "Let's go!" sent the Big Reds into formation to receive the kickoff.

Chip stood poised nervously on the five-yard line, watching the Prep kicker raise his arms and then start his short, chopping steps toward the ball. The blue-clad wave of expectant tacklers picked up the cadence and then dashed swiftly downfield on the thump of the ball. It was a good kick, with plenty of force and height. Chip figured it for the ten-yard line and remained motionless as his teammates charged eagerly forward to meet the Prep tacklers. Just as the ball seemed destined to fall to the ground untouched, Chip sprinted ahead and took it waist-high on the dead run. One quick glance was all he needed to see that the Prep flanks were well protected, so he headed straight up the field, right for the middle of the wedge his teammates had formed.

A PASS AND A PRAYER

It was the Prep fullback, the kicker, who met the wedge head-on and piled up the Big Reds interference on the thirty-yard line. Chip was hit hard from both sides and downed on the thirty-five.

"Nice blocking, guys," Chip said crisply. "Now we'll give 'em a little of their own medicine! Heads up! Spread formation! Pass! One-one hundred on twenty-two! Fan out! Break!"

The student-packed stands buzzed again as the Big Reds dashed out of the huddle and spread across the field, almost from sideline to sideline. In the center of the field, tall Nick Trullo straddled the ball with two reserves taking up the guard spots. Chris Badger was a yard or two behind Trullo, a little to the right, in the back position, with Hilton about ten to twelve yards directly behind the ball. Near the left side, Soapy Smith and Biggie Cohen were on the line with Speed Morris about five yards back.

Halfway between the ball and the right sideline, the two guards and the right tackle, Lou Mazotta, were on the scrimmage line, while Red Schwartz, the seventh man the rules require on the line of scrimmage, was several yards from the right sideline smack in front of the Prep bleachers. Husky Cody Collins was about five yards behind Schwartz. That meant Smith and Schwartz, left and right ends respectively, as well as Hilton's three backfield mates were eligible pass receivers.

The Prep students had been waiting for the spread formation, and now those in the know began explaining what it was all about.

"That's the formation I was tellin' you about! Watch this! Watch that quarterback!"

"Bet it's a fake! Bet he runs with the ball!"

"Could be, but he usually passes from this formation. Look how far back he is from the line of scrimmage."

"Can't run from that setup. Wouldn't have any inter-ference."

"Oh, no! Look how the defense has spread out too. It would be almost like running in an open field."

The action on the field settled the debates. Hilton started toward the right, in motion, before the ball was snapped. It was a deceptive move because it seemed that Trullo could snap the ball only to Chris Badger. At the snap, several Prep linemen fell for the deception and charged toward the stocky Big Reds fullback. But Nick Trullo could spiral a football from center almost as hard as he could serve up a fastball from the pitcher's mound, and the ball came spinning back to the right of the speed-ing Valley Falls captain.

Chip caught the ball on the dead run and in six quick steps was behind his two guards and the right tackle who'd dropped back to give him pass protection. Dancing there behind the linemen and watching his receivers fan out, Chip faked and feinted until he was almost sur-rounded by charging Prep linemen. Then he hurled the ball far down the left sideline ahead of Speed.

Morris had cut toward the center of the field, re-versed direction, and then used his change of pace to race ahead and get behind the Prep defensive back. The throw looked high and long, almost as if it would fly out of bounds. But Chip knew how fast Speed could move his powerful legs. Hilton could hang a football on a clothes-line, and that's the way he hung this one out for Morris. He took it at finger-tip height without breaking stride, and that was all there was to it! Speed easily outdis-tanced his pursuers for the touchdown.

Sometimes, a sports technique is so perfectly exe-cuted it brings spontaneous shouts of appreciation from the spectators. Other times, the fans are so absorbed in the play and its execution that they're left speechless. That's the way the Prep fans reacted: the crowd sat in awed silence. This was too much. This Valley Falls team was too good!

But they were good sports and watched the rest of the scrimmage, cheering the good plays and admiring the perfection of the visitors' attack and defense. Now the Prep passes, which had clicked so well when the Big Reds backfield regulars were on the sidelines, were batted down or intercepted. Hilton, Morris, Badger, and Collins covered the passing areas like a blanket.

Soapy Smith declared he'd rather play football than eat. But his teammates and friends lifted knowing eyebrows every time Soapy made the comment. Under pressure, Soapy sometimes reluctantly admitted he might not be the best football player in the state, but he was runner-up to no one when it came to food, which he proved after the scrimmage in Midwestern's oak-paneled dining hall.

Rockwell, seated at a center table with the headmaster, several members of the Prep faculty, and Coach Bill Richards, made a show of enjoying the meal. But he was glad when it was time to climb wearily aboard the bus and head for Valley Falls. He knew he was good and sick, but he also knew it was nothing his old pal Doc Jones couldn't knock out of him.

Just as the team was boarding the bus, he saw Chip and Biggie lifting Josh Connors up the steps, and he forgot all about his own illness. The busy black eyes spotted Josh's taped leg and quickly checked with Pop Brown.

"What's the matter with Connors, Pop?"

"Why . . . er . . . he's got a bad leg, Rock. Got clipped this after—"

"Clipped? When did it happen? Why, he didn't even play! Couldn't have been clipped."

Pop nodded firmly. "Did, Coach. Got clipped. Nothing broke, just some bad muscles. The Prep doctor checked him out."

"But how did it happen, Pop? How?"

Pop's steady eyes conveyed much more than his answer. "Coach Brasher knows all about it, Coach. He could tell you exactly how it happened."

Rockwell, holding Connors by the arm, asked, "How did it happen, Josh?"

But Connors stuttered before answering and was so evasive that Rockwell knew the spirited little quarterback was covering up. In his usual understanding manner, the veteran coach patted Connors softly on the back and turned away. But he nodded knowingly when he looked once more into Pop Brown's eyes and spoke softly to the trainer.

"I see," he said thoughtfully. "I see. Sure it's only the muscles, Pop? Well, we'll take him to see Doc Jones soon as we get home. Want to see Doc myself."

At that moment, Tom Brasher and Jerry Davis were enjoying two thick steaks at Jerry's favorite restaurant and talking about Rockwell. The two men were completely different in appearance and style. But they were united by a college friendship that had lasted since graduation, and Davis had been trying for years to maneuver Brasher into a job on the Valley Falls High School faculty.

Davis, oldest son of the owner of Valley Falls's leading jewelry store, was a sports fanatic. He'd never played sports, never been on any team other than for a short stint as a student manager of his college football team. That brief taste had been enough to qualify him, in his personal opinion, as a sports expert. He was envious of successful athletes and desperately wanted to control Valley Falls's athletic programs and coaching staff. Jerry was probably the best "armchair" coach and second-guesser in the state.

He hated Henry Rockwell with all the frustrated venom of his nature, chiefly because Rockwell had recognized him as a phony and wouldn't allow him to interfere in the school's athletic program. But Davis was popular with the younger business people in Valley Falls, and he had used these friendships to slowly but continually undermine Rockwell. In fact, Davis talked of little else, and his conversation at dinner this evening was no different. He leaned over his plate and spoke to Brasher in low tones.

"Tom," he said earnestly, "every day's important. Every day! We gotta get rid of him this fall. We need a young man in charge at the high school, and you're it. That's why I put pressure on the mayor to give you the recreation job and then this position at school as the assistant coach. You're booked solid for Rockwell's spot if we play our cards right. You making any progress with the kids on the team?"

Brasher nodded. "Sure am," he said confidently. "I gave one a good going-over today. I'm building up their respect for my own football ability first, and then I'll hit them with my plays and stuff."

Davis nodded, but his face was serious as he cautioned Brasher. "Look, Tom, you gotta be sure to control your temper. Take it easy with the kids. If you do your part, Muddy and I will do ours and we can't lose. Just keep your head. OK?"

Brasher nodded, but his face clouded slightly, and Davis noticed it. "You havin' trouble with Rockwell or Stewart?" Davis asked.

"Naw, I can handle them, easy. Looks like I'll have to take that Hilton kid down a few notches though. He's too smart for his own good."

Davis nodded grimly. "I know," he said. "I guess that kid bothers me almost as much as Rockwell."

Brasher's jaws were clamped so tightly together lumps of muscles formed on each side of his face. "I'll take care of that show-off," he gritted. "Soon too."

"Won't bother me any," Davis replied shortly. "Only thing is you've got to be careful. Hilton's popular in Valley Falls."

Davis changed the subject. "How do you like Rockwell's spin-T formation?"

"It's terrible!" Brasher said vehemently. "These has-been high school coaches are all alike. They get scared they're gonna lose their jobs, so they try something screwy. Just because some guy had a lot of material and won a championship with some kind of a new offense, they think they're gonna do the same thing. Me, I like the old-school football—straight, hard-running football. That's why I stick with something that works."

"He won the state last year," Davis said dryly, "and some of his plays seem pretty good."

Brasher snorted. "Mothball stuff. Those plays are worthless, and so is he!"

"Well," Davis said resignedly, "you'll have a tough time selling Rockwell on anything except his own stuff. He's hardheaded. Why, I could've won a lot of championships for the old goat with just three or four players if he'd let me bring in transfers."

Brasher's head shot up abruptly. "Speakin' of transfers, I wish I could get a kid by the name of Rankin here. He's a *real* quarterback. Two hundred pounds, experienced, and loves hard football. He'd run circles around Hilton."

"Wouldn't have a chance, Tom. Rockwell wouldn't hold still for it. He's dead set against transfers. Anyway, where would the kid live?"

"With his family. The old man's out of work. He'd move to Valley Falls in a minute if we could get him a job."

"The mayor could fix that easily enough, but it wouldn't be any use. Rockwell wouldn't let him play."

"Not even if the mayor put pressure on him?"

"You don't know Rockwell. No one puts pressure on him. Has his standards and sticks to them. He's been here a long time, Tom, and he's got a lot of friends. Important friends in the whole community. They actually respect the old man."

"But Condon runs the school board, doesn't he? He's the mayor."

"Condon runs nearly everything in this town, my friend, and everyone in the school system except Henry Rockwell. Rockwell's stubborn. He won't listen to anyone. Wait till you get to know him!"

"Who wants to know the old has-been! Suit me if I never saw him again!"

"Muddy and I are sure with you there, Tom. We have to orchestrate some way to get rid of him. Just have to!"

"Maybe I got a plan," Brasher clipped, his voice hard and cold. "A plan to kill two birds with one stone."

Three's a Crowd!

WHILE BRASHER and Davis were venting their anger, Rockwell was in Doc Jones's office, undergoing a thorough examination, and downstairs, directly under the popular physician's office, Chip Hilton was working at his job at the Sugar Bowl.

Chip had worked for John Schroeder, owner of the Sugar Bowl, for several years ever since Chip's father had been killed in an accident at the pottery. The money Chip earned helped out at home, added to his college fund, and, perhaps more importantly, helped him appreciate his mom's determined efforts to provide for them in Big Chip's absence. He admired her courage and self-reliance and the example she'd set for him through her career as a supervisor at the telephone company.

Two of Chip's good friends were also employed by John Schroeder: Soapy Smith and Petey Jackson, the skinny fountain manager. They were discussing the afternoon scrimmage during the early evening business lull.

"You say this Brasher clipped Josh?" Petey asked.

Soapy nodded. "Sure did! Chip took care of Brasher later, without even knowin' it though. But good!"

"Where'd Brasher come from anyway?"

"Someplace in Illinois. S'posed to have been an All-American and played pro."

"Wonder where Rock met him?"

"He didn't. Didn't even know him!" Soapy declared. "The school board hired him. School board hires all the teachers."

"You mean Rockwell doesn't even pick his own assistants? Doesn't seem right!"

"Lots of things don't seem right and lots of things ain't right."

"Rock's the head of the department, isn't he?"

"Yeah, sure, but the school board hires the teachers."

"You mean the principal doesn't have any say about hiring the teachers!"

"Nope! Not a thing. Just the mayor and the board. It don't take no mental wizard to figure out how come Brasher was hired. Not with Jerry Davis's old man on the board, and Jerry and Brasher pals. Everybody knows Jerry got the mayor to appoint Brasher to the Recreation Department last July."

"How come he got to be a coach?"

"Easy. When Bill Thomas quit, Jerry got Mayor Condon to put Brasher in the Physical Education Department and make him assistant football coach. He's smooth."

"Sounds to me like he could mean trouble!" Petey ventured.

"Anyone who's a friend of Jerry Davis means trouble," Soapy said sourly. "Especially for the Rock. For Chip, too, after what happened this afternoon. Chip sure made Brasher look bad."

"Speed told me Brasher was burned plenty," Petey said gleefully.

Soapy changed the subject. "Man," he said admiringly, "you shoulda seen what Chip did to the Preppies!"

"What's Midwestern got?" Petey asked.

Soapy crammed another spoonful of ice cream into his mouth and grinned. "Well," he drawled, between mouthfuls, "they got a great campus and great buildings and great uniforms, and they got a great training table, and the food's outta this world." He smacked his lips and rolled his eyes. "And, that's what's wrong with them! They got it too easy!"

"Yeah," Petey agreed pointedly, "and that's what's wrong with you! Bet you've put on twenty pounds since you came to work here."

That hurt. The one real problem in Soapy's life was his weight. He halted the ice-cream-filled spoon halfway between the plate and his mouth as his panic-stricken eyes met Petey's scornful gaze. "You think I have, Petey? You really think I have?" He searched desperately and unsuccessfully through his pockets and then smiled gratefully when Petey flipped a coin toward him.

"No!" Soapy's pained voice rang out. "No! Can't be! Two hundred! No! These scales right?"

"Tested every week!"

Soapy glowered at the scale and then placed the half-emptied dish of ice cream on the counter. Looking at it longingly, he sighed and then reluctantly pushed it away. "I don't really like the stuff," he managed. "Just read somewhere it was good for athletes."

Eldon "Muddy" Waters, new sports editor for the *Valley Times,* jerked the paper from the printer and added it to several others on his desk. "There," he said vindictively, "that ought to give 'em something to talk about. Wait until they get an eyeful of that!"

He glanced at the clock on the wall, noted it was ten o'clock, sighed contentedly, and moved briskly toward the door. He had time for a fast sandwich, and then he'd run out to football practice at Ohlsen Stadium and work up something for his Sunday column. He decided to stop by the jewelry store and pick up Jerry Davis.

People in Valley Falls, like in most small towns, were friendly—quick to greet friends, acquaintances, even total strangers. This sunny Saturday morning in September brought brisk, cool temperatures, which made everyone hustle a little bit more and call hello with more energy. Yet, if someone had followed Muddy Waters's progress up Main Street and noted the few greetings, the averted heads, and the lack of warmth given the sportswriter, he would have been surprised. What kind of man could arouse such extreme animosity in his first few months in Valley Falls?

Muddy Waters was about thirty years old, slender, and rather average-looking. His pale-blue eyes constantly shifted from one thing to another. Impatient and lacking concentration, he seldom remained still very long. He had come to Valley Falls shortly before the arrival of Tom Brasher to replace the *Valley Times's* veteran sports editor, Joe Kennedy. Many people were surprised to learn Waters was one of Jerry Davis's friends.

Waters's friendship for Davis soon became evident in his sports reporting. He gave Jerry Davis's favorite sports projects plenty of positive ink and vigorously attacked the people and programs his new friend opposed. Rockwell became the columnist's chief target. That was a mistake, especially in the eyes of Valley Falls's older residents. Henry Rockwell was a tradition, a fixture in Big

Reds athletics, one of the trusted and dependable. Older sports fans resented "Waters's impudence."

But their dislike and coolness didn't bother the newcomer. He swaggered along Main Street this Saturday morning, unconcerned by the people's attitude, and barged into Davis's big jewelry store where Jerry greeted him warmly. By 10:30, the two associates were seated in the bleachers, watching the Big Reds warm up.

Davis glanced at his watch. "Late," he said, in a surprised voice. "Rockwell usually starts at ten o'clock sharp. Don't see Tom either. Wonder what's wrong?"

Waters didn't reply. He was unfamiliar with the precision and to-the-minute schedule Rockwell always maintained.

"Something's up," Davis worried. "You suppose the Rock and Tom are having it out?"

Waters shrugged his shoulders. "Got me," he said briefly. "Wouldn't know. Guess Tom can handle himself though."

Jerry Davis was right. Rockwell and Brasher were having it out, or rather Rockwell was having it out with Brasher. Doc Jones had ordered the coach to stay in bed Saturday morning, but he had tossed and turned all night thinking about his new backfield coach. When morning came, he dressed and went to his office. The moment Brasher arrived, Pop Brown advised the surprised new assistant he was wanted upstairs in the office, and the two of them had been there ever since.

Jerry Davis wasn't the only person disturbed by Rockwell's tardiness. Chet Stewart, Rockwell's chief assistant and the coach of the Big Reds line, kept the boys busy, but his eyes constantly shifted toward the gym. He knew his boss was sick and should be home in bed, and he was worried about the meeting taking place in Rock's office.

A PASS AND A PRAYER

On the field, the regulars showed their impatience by charging a bit too quickly as they ran signals and by occasional muttered remarks. It was hard to fool kids. They had seen this showdown between Rockwell and Brasher coming. But it was the Big Reds captain, Chip Hilton, who was on the right track and was fully aware of the implications in the close friendship of Tom Brasher, Muddy Waters, and Jerry Davis. Chip figured the trio spelled trouble for Henry Rockwell. But he kept his views to himself and listened to his teammates.

"What d'ya think they're talking about?"

"S'pose it's because of Josh?"

"Sure. Josh and some of that other stuff he's been doin'."

"Hey, how's Josh anyway?"

"It's only a sprain!"

"Hope the Rock lays it on Brasher good."

"Chip laid it on him!"

"Big time! I can still see him sprawling in front of all the Prep players."

"Maybe that's why he sneaked out right after the scrimmage."

"Pop said Rock didn't look too good, looked sick."

"Drop it! Here they come!"

Rockwell and Brasher came slowly out of the locker room, down the steps leading past the stadium, and then across the practice field. Neither spoke, and the tension between the two was clearly evident. Brasher was red-faced as he stalked along with arrogance and anger. His temper was apparent in his hunched shoulders and his scuffing feet. Rockwell was pale but clearly in command of the situation. He beckoned to Stewart.

"Chet," Rockwell said wearily, "I've got an appointment. Suppose you take over practice. Go over the signals first, then through all the plays. I guess the boys are loosened up enough after yesterday's scrimmage. See you Monday."

While the players were scrambling up the bleachers, Chet and Pop Brown set up the whiteboard. Brasher joined Davis and Waters, and they moved up to the top row away from the players. Then Stewart took charge, and the talking quieted as the stocky line coach worked at the board.

Stewart pointed to the circles he had drawn and spoke slowly and distinctly. "I know you've heard all this before, but we'll review it anyway. Keep in mind one of

(E) 36 (T) 12 (G) 8 (C) 8 (G) 12 (T) 36 (E)

the Rock's favorite sayings: 'Repetition is the key to success.' It's a good one."

There was a snicker from high up in the back of the bleachers. Stewart's face flushed scarlet. He stopped dead still, and his eyes shot directly toward Brasher and his two sneering companions. For a second, it seemed Chet was on the verge of saying something to them, but after a short pause, he continued. It was obvious to everyone he was upset.

"The small mark in front of C is the ball. Keep in mind that the line of scrimmage is defined by the length of the ball and extends all the way from sideline to sideline. Neither team may encroach upon this little strip before the ball is snapped, without being offsides.

A PASS AND A PRAYER

"Naturally, the circle containing the C represents the center, those with the G's the guards, the T's the tackles, and the E's the ends. The figures between each circle represent inches and are important because those distances—eight inches between the center and each guard, twelve inches between the guards and the tackles, and thirty-six inches between the tackles and the ends—mean the formation is set up right for our plays. Spacing is important because it has a lot to do with the timing and blocking assignments."

Stewart erased the marks from the board and expertly outlined Rockwell's T-formation.

"Circle 1 is the quarterback, 3 is the fullback, and 2 and 4 are the halfbacks. The quarterback must stand so

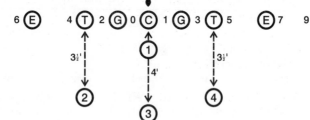

his arms contact the center with his hands extending down between the center's legs.

"The fullback is four feet back, and the halfbacks are three and a half feet behind the line.

"Chip and Nick come down here and show us the correct center-quarterback positions. . . . That's fine. Note how close Chip has his hands to the ball, and yet his back is straight and his head is up, and he's in a position to see the defense. He never looks down at the ball, just straight ahead. Thanks.

"Note the numbers beside each lineman. They designate the hole through or around which the ball carrier is expected to go, even numbers to the left, odd numbers to the right. This probably was the first system ever used in numbering the holes on the line, but it's still as good as any.

"Now we'll call a play. Remember, the quarterback handles the ball on every play in this series. The first digit of the first number called represents the back: number 1 for the quarterback, 2 for the left halfback. The second digit of the first number represents the hole, the numbers next to the linemen.

"S'pose we say 21, Hillie. Where would the play go, and who would carry the ball?"

Jarrod Hill stood up and answered promptly, "That would be the left halfback just to the right of center."

"Good! Now answer these as quickly as possible. I'll call 'em fast! 34?"

"Fullback off left tackle!"

"48?"

"Right half around left end!"

"35?"

"Fullback off right tackle!"

"19?"

"Quarterback around right end!"

"Good! Now, Hillie, suppose Chip should call this signal: 39-26-48-72-51-97."

Hillie's reply came almost as quick as the question. "That would be the fullback—Chris, that is—around right end with the left half—Speed, that is—in motion toward the right, and the ball would be passed on the sixth number!"

A PASS AND A PRAYER

"That's right, Hillie," Stewart said, "but why would Speed be in motion?"

"Because the second number begins with 2. When the second number begins with 2, 4, or 3, for that matter, it means that man will be in motion."

"Good! What's a flanker?"

"Well, in our system, the fullback, number 3, is always the flanker. The flanker usually takes a position outside the defensive end and a yard or so back, depending on the play."

Stewart smiled and nodded in a pleased manner. "Nice going, Hillie."

A false cough came from behind the players from the top row of the bleachers, and through every player's mind flashed the thought that Brasher had made the sarcastic sound deliberately. The guys watched Coach Stewart for a reaction, but Chet's face was impassive, and after a second's pause he continued.

"Now we come to the snap or starting signal. That number is important chiefly because it gives you the jump on the defense. You know ahead of time when the ball's going to be snapped. Now in Rock's system—"

Again there was a cough followed by a snicker and a half-smothered laugh from high up in the bleachers. This time, Stewart stopped and walked to the left, directly below but in front of the trio on the top row. The air was charged with electricity, and the players knew Chet had taken all he would take from Brasher and his two mimicking friends. But they admired Chet's self-control and the calmness in his voice.

"This is an important practice. I'll have to ask you outsiders to leave. I'm sorry."

Brasher's face turned red, and his voice trembled with rage. "They're with me, Stewart," he said angrily, "and they'll leave when I say."

Stewart's voice was still calm and firm. "That's all right, Brasher, but they're disturbing practice. If you want to talk to them while we're working, you'll have to take them somewhere else, somewhere out of hearing."

A long, tense moment followed. Stewart held his position, his jaw clamped firmly and his eyes unwavering as he waited. It was Brasher who cracked, muttering to his two companions and leading them down from the top row of bleachers, clattering noisily and deliberately down the steps. They moved across the field toward the big concrete stadium. Stewart continued as if nothing had happened.

"Now, in Rock's system, the second digit of the second number tells you on what number the center snaps the ball. Smith, s'pose you stand up and call out on what number the ball will be snapped. Ready? 45?"

"On the fifth number Chip calls."

"33?"

"Third number called."

"64?"

"Fourth number called."

"Thanks, Soapy. Now for the plays."

CHAPTER 4

Working with Kids

TOM BRASHER had an evil temper. For the second time that morning, he had been chastised for his behavior, and he responded with burning rage. "Can you imagine that jerk?" he demanded belligerently. "Can you imagine him havin' the guts to pull something like this in front of all those kids?" He turned to Davis. "It's a good thing you held me back, or I'd have taken that guy apart right then. I might do it yet!"

Davis and Waters exchanged glances. Then Waters expressed both men's thoughts. "Look, Tom," he said in a soothing voice, "we know how you feel, and we know what you're up against, but flying off the handle isn't going to help. Look, you've just got to control your temper until we get rid of Rockwell and you're put in charge. Then you can put the heat on Stewart and do whatever you want. Right now, we've got to play it smart. Jerry and I were talking things over this morning. We're making great progress, and we'll be successful if you control yourself. What happened in Rockwell's office this morning?"

Brasher banged his broad hand down on the fence railing he was leaning on, and his voice increased with anger as he talked.

"It was all I could do to keep from punchin' him. Keeps me up there an hour, talkin' about the ethics of coaching and how a coach has to protect kids and all that baloney. Said I was too rough. Said I wasn't hired to demonstrate my playin' ability. How dare he talk to me like that!"

Brasher spread his hands out in front of his bulky body innocently. "Talked as if I'd been showin' off!"

Waters's pale-blue eyes were puzzled. "What caused all this?"

Brasher shrugged contemptuously. "Yesterday, when I was tryin' to speed up the reserve backs, I chased Connors around end and tackled him. The kid puts on an act like he's hurt, and the old goat saw it or else that stooge of his—that jerk Stewart—saw it and shot off his big mouth."

"What else did Rockwell say?" Waters prodded.

"Said he hoped I'd realize the things he was tellin' me were for my own good. That coaching was a great responsibility and most boys got closer to a coach than to their parents—all that sentimental junk. Then he had the brass to tell me he knew I'd like it here in Valley Falls, and he hoped we could be friends. Can you believe it?"

"You shake hands with him?" Waters asked.

Brasher laughed boisterously. "With him? What do you think? When he stuck out his hand, I just walked out of the office. Shake hands? No way! Not with Rockwell! Not in a million years!"

A PASS AND A PRAYER

"Maybe you oughta take it a little slower," Davis warned. "Remember, we aren't ready yet. We've got to give Muddy a chance to swing the fans your way. You better play ball with him for a couple of weeks."

"Jerry's right, Tom," Waters said, nodding his head in agreement. "Stay cool. Play it smart. Go along with the guy until we get a break. Remember, he's got a veteran team. All we need is for something to go wrong in one of the games. In the meantime, I'll take a few digs at him in the paper along with that smart-aleck Hilton kid, and when the time's right, we'll all hit him at once."

A little later, Davis and Waters left, and Brasher rejoined the squad in the bleachers. Soon afterward, Stewart sent the squad jogging around the field for "three laps and in!"

Petey Jackson was the first Sugar Bowl employee to see the *Times* that afternoon, and he dashed away from his post behind the counter as if he were, indeed, the halfback he insisted he could have been.

"Hey, Chip, Soapy! Look at this! What's with Waters?" Chip and Soapy looked at the article.

TIMES AND SPORTS
By Muddy Waters

Yesterday, I witnessed a preview of this year's Valley Falls football team. Unless some changes are made in the Big Reds' attack, last year's state champions are going to lose their laurels. Why?

Because Henry Rockwell has deliberately built his entire offense around one player—Chip Hilton. What if Hilton gets injured? Furthermore, does Rockwell think the other coaches in Section Two will let him get away with a one-man offense?

How about the other members of Rockwell's veteran backfield? Maybe they'd like to carry the ball once or twice during a game. No, it's all Hilton. He's the quarterback and calls all the plays.

Speaking of plays, Rockwell's spin-T attack is entirely devoid of sound football principles. Deception is important in any football style, but most coaches combine it with solid football.

Question: Why not let backfield coach Tom Brasher add a few of the famous Tigers's plays to the team's repertoire? Coach Brasher was the backfield star of that great pro team and undoubtedly knows the famous Tigers's attack by heart.

Midwestern's air attack clicked time and again during one stage of the scrimmage. Rockwell had better devise a better defense against aerials. Bill Richards, new Prep coach, was satisfied with his starting backfield but worried about his forward wall.

Tom Brasher, new Big Reds backfield coach, turned down a fabulous pro coaching offer to remain in Valley Falls. He prefers working with kids and intends to make it his lifework. The Big Reds are lucky to add this big-time player and coach to their aging staff. Coach Brasher brings modern, up-to-date football to Valley Falls.

"Chipper, do you know this jerk?"

Chip shook his head. "No," he said worriedly. "I never saw him in my life until this morning when he came out to practice with Jerry Davis."

"That explains it!" Petey snapped. "Anyone who hangs around with that guy, with that Davis, is a jerk, big time. No wonder he's against the Rock."

A PASS AND A PRAYER

"'Up-to-date football' expert!" Soapy said sarcastically. "Hah, he couldn't carry Rock's shoes. 'Prefers workin' with kids!' Hah! Workin' 'em over maybe. If what he did to Josh is his idea of workin' with kids, I can't wait to see what happens when he 'works with' Biggie!"

The persistent ringing of the telephone broke up the conversation. Petey Jackson got there first, explaining pointedly that it probably was "one of his babes." But it wasn't one of Petey's "babes." Instead, Mary Hilton asked to speak with her son.

"Chip, have you heard about Coach Rockwell? Well, he's very sick. They took him to the hospital a little while ago. I'll see if I can find out more before you come home."

Mary Hilton was waiting for Chip in the family room, trying to figure out the reason for Muddy Waters's campaign against Henry Rockwell and the writer's references to her son. Chip's mom was interested in all of his activities, and she knew sports were the big thing in her son's life.

Ever since the death of Chip's father, Mary Hilton had tried to fill the dual role of mother and father. The mother part came easily enough, but it had required real genius to develop the correct attitude toward sports and a growing boy's interests and problems. They had developed a wonderful relationship, sharing their successes and disappointments as a team.

Chip's quick footsteps on the front porch brought Mary Hilton to her feet, and she met her son in the hall. One glance was all she needed to see that Chip was worried.

"You hear anything more about the coach, Mom?"

"Yes, Chip, he's in the hospital with some sort of virus. Doc Jones says it's serious, says he may be hospitalized for weeks."

Chip groaned. "Oh, no! How's Mrs. Rockwell? Mom, what are we going to do? What's going to happen to the team?"

She tried to reassure Chip, but even Hoops and his best feline antics had no effect. Chip was still dejected and worried when he went to bed. He couldn't sleep most of the night. Early Sunday morning, all the Big Reds regulars turned up at the Hilton home, one by one, all slightly embarrassed, but determined to share their concern. Chip felt as awkward as his teammates, but the tension was broken by the town's fire siren. A quick phone check located the fire at the high school baseball field. That broke up the gloom. Speed's Mustang, loaded with his loyal friends, careened to the scene of excitement.

At the fire, while the fire department was working to extinguish the small blaze under one of the stands, the Big Reds gave advice from the sidelines and kidded one another.

The mayor's arrival attracted the athletes' attention, and most of the remarks came from them. Mayor Condon wasn't too popular with most of the teenagers and with many of the adults. However, he was extremely popular with certain groups and had been smart enough to promote their support. Condon had been slick enough to realize the residents of Valley Falls in their twenties and thirties carried most of the voting strength. So Condon played up to them and won his election chiefly through their support. Jerry Davis had been one of Condon's most vigorous campaigners, and the mayor hadn't forgotten. In fact, he and Davis were friends.

Later that afternoon, after church, the Hilton backyard "Athletic Club" had a full turnout. Sundays were always important to Chip and his friends. On nice days they assembled in the backyard, on the basketball court that Big Chip Hilton had built for Little Chip years before, and during bad weather, they took over the family room in the house. Some mothers might have been inconvenienced by having a bunch of teenagers all over the house but not Mrs. Hilton. She welcomed Chip's friends any day and any time. In fact, she got a great kick out of seeing her son surrounded by his carefree and happy friends in their home.

With the fire over, Chip and his friends were in a solemn mood. Rockwell's illness, Muddy Waters's critical review of the scrimmage with Midwestern, his direct criticism of Chip, and the Brasher episode had confused and annoyed them. They were an angry, frustrated group of athletes. Soapy Smith was the most garrulous.

"What's eatin' this Waters?" Soapy demanded. "Where'd he come from? Why did he have to choose Valley Falls? What's he got against Chip? What's he got against the Rock? What's he after anyway?"

Red Schwartz scoffed. "What's he after? You know what he's after as well as anyone else—the Rock! Him and Davis and the rest of that crew."

"You'd think he'd lay off when Rock's sick," Biggie Cohen stated bitterly. "You see his column today?"

No one answered. They had all seen the *Times*. The front page had carried a nice story about Rockwell's illness, but there wasn't anything nice in Muddy Waters's column. He'd raised Rockwell's age and the state retirement clause and stressed "football was a young man's game." But that wasn't all. He'd again attacked the team, criticized Rockwell's plays, and slammed Chip Hilton's "selfish play."

The *Post* had also carried a front page and a sports page story about Rockwell. But both stories had been positive. Pete Williams, sports editor of the *Post,* devoted his whole column to Rockwell, citing the great record of his football teams and predicting the current team would be one of the veteran coach's best. Williams ended his column with the statement, "Rockwell, flat on his back and in the hospital, could still do a better job of coaching football than any high school coach in the United States."

Jerry Davis's and Muddy Waters's ears should have been burning at that moment. But the two schemers seemed totally unaware of burning ears or any other superstition as they sat with Tom Brasher in Jerry's car and plotted further trouble for Henry Rockwell.

"This is our big break, Jerry," Waters said eagerly. "We can't miss! All you gotta do is have Condon work on the principal. What's his name? Zimmerman? And have Condon appoint Tom acting head coach. That's a must! Now that Rockwell's out of the picture for the season— let's hope!"

Davis nodded doubtfully. "Yes, sure, Muddy, but what about Stewart? He's next in line and Rockwell left him in charge. You heard him."

"So? Condon runs the school! He'll do anything you want. All you gotta do is ask! Right?"

Davis agreed reluctantly. "Yes, maybe." He turned to Brasher. "How does it strike you, Tom?"

Brasher laughed derisively. "What do you think? If I ever get in charge of that club—"

"But what about Stewart?" Davis persisted. "What if he won't take it lying down?"

"He'll take it," Brasher stated harshly. "If Zimmerman says I'm in charge, well, I'm in charge."

Waters moved impatiently. "What are we waiting for?" he demanded shortly. "There's no time like the present. Let's see Condon right now!"

CHAPTER 5

Acting Head Coach

PRINCIPAL ZIMMERMAN was surprised when Mayor Condon called, asking him to lunch. But after the first rush of pleasure, he began to speculate about the reason. "He must want me to do something," Zimmerman muttered, "something I probably won't want to do. Wonder what he wants?"

Zimmerman didn't know it, but his mind was being made up for him right at that moment by Condon. And Muddy Waters was already planning the scoop for the next issue of the *Times*. Condon picked Zimmerman up at the high school at noon. The smooth politician soon dissipated the principal's fears. The mayor was a perfect host, and by the time they were having coffee, Zimmerman was completely off guard. Then Condon went to work.

"Too bad about Rockwell," Condon offered sympathetically. "Of course, he's slowing up, and something like this was bound to occur sooner or later, but you hate to see it happen, just the same.

"You know, I've been thinking about Rockwell and his successor a lot lately. Sort of a premonition, I guess. He's past retirement age, and we've got to be thinking about someone to take over when he stops coaching. This sudden illness may be a blessing in disguise, that is, if we put it to good use."

Zimmerman was wary now, and his voice was pitched just a shade above normal when he spoke. "What do you have in mind, Mayor?" He realized he'd just walked into the mayor's setup.

"Well, Zimmerman, nothing special. I was just going to suggest you appoint the new assistant, Tom Brasher, acting head coach while Rockwell is sick. Be a good chance for us to see what he can do."

Zimmerman shook his head uncertainly. "I don't think Rockwell would like that, Mayor. You see, he turned the team over to Chet Stewart. Chet's been here several years, and he's been Hank's first assistant right along."

"Well, I don't think Henry would mind if you changed that, Zim. After all, it's your job to make the assignments, you know."

The mayor studied Zimmerman covertly, saw that the man was trying to devise an argument, and quickly followed up his advantage. Condon believed in keeping an opponent off balance. "Brasher's sort of a protégé of mine, Zim," he said confidentially. "I was kinda set on him taking over when Rockwell retires. Now, you just run along and do as I say, and if there are any repercussions, refer them to me. I'll be glad to help."

Zimmerman was whipped. He couldn't even get close to Condon's aggressiveness. "Would it be all right if I made the change tomorrow?" he asked, trying to delay the unpleasant task as long as possible.

Condon was gracious and pleasant. "Why, of course, Zim," he responded warmly, patting Zimmerman on the back. "That'll be just fine." He slipped his arm affectionately around the principal's shoulders. "And, Zim," he continued, "I want you to know I appreciate your cooperation. I won't forget it."

That afternoon, Stewart began practice by assembling the squad in the bleachers and reading the practice outline Rockwell had prepared earlier in the season.

"We'll follow the outlines just as Coach laid them out, and when he gets back, we'll be right on schedule. Guess you all know Rock is pretty sick. I was at the hospital, and they let me see him for a couple of minutes. He sends his regards and said for all of you to get in shape because when he gets out, he'll be rarin' to go."

Stewart swallowed hard and looked down at the ground before continuing. His emotion was apparent to every member of the squad, and everyone there empathized with him. Chet's loyalty to Rockwell was legendary with Big Reds athletes, and they respected him even more for his quiet display of genuine emotion.

Chip glanced at Brasher. The new backfield coach was looking at Stewart with a smirk on his lips and with disgust apparent in his expression. A surge of dislike swept Chip so intensely his hands shook. But he stilled the impulse for action and concentrated on Stewart's words.

"All right, now, let's go to work. I'll take the guards and tackles for group work, and Coach Brasher will handle the centers, ends, and backs and work on the plays. Let's go!"

Chip led the backs to Brasher's side and moved into his usual position at quarterback behind big Nick Trullo.

ACTING HEAD COACH

Chris Badger was at full, Speed at left half, and Cody Collins was in the right halfback spot.

The reserve backfield lined up with Spike Davis over the ball, Dan Harding at quarter, Bill Carroll at full, and with Jordan Taylor and Bob Blaine at the halves.

"All right," Brasher shouted harshly, "start movin'! You guys pose like you're rock stars! Let's at least *look* like football players!"

After a half-hour running signals, Brasher's shrill whistle brought the backfield coach's squad hustling to surround him in a tight little circle. When the guys quieted, he began speaking in the quick, sharp voice he affected on the field.

"Just for a change, now, we'll try a *real* football formation—the single wing. You know what the single wing is? All right, then snap to it. We'll use the same signals, and I'll give you the plays as we go. You reserves run the same play as the regulars.

"We'll hit off-tackle first. Shift to the right. Schwartz, you and Collins are s'posed to work on the defensive tackle and drive him in. You take the end, Hilton. With a line, of course, the runnin' guard might team up with you to block him to the outside. Badger, you lead the play, and I *mean* lead it. Morris, you get the ball on a direct pass from center, and I want you to be movin' when you get the ball. Everyone got it? OK, let's go!"

Chip called the play, a bit reluctantly and a bit doubtfully, because Rockwell was strictly for the *T*. He could tell by his teammates' grumbling they weren't feeling too good about this sudden change in offensive formation either.

And they had company. Chet Stewart had caught the change in formation and had watched them with puzzled eyes until he caught on. Then he came trotting across the field. "Hey," he said, looking from Brasher to the players and back again, "what goes? We don't use anything like that. Come on, stick to the practice outline."

"Wait a minute, Stewart," Brasher commanded menacingly. "Who's coachin' this backfield?"

Stewart looked at Brasher in amazement. He was completely unprepared for Brasher's opposition and for a moment couldn't speak. Then he spoke slowly and calmly.

"You're the backfield coach, Brasher," he said evenly, "but Rockwell is the head coach, and he planned the offense we're going to use." Stewart paused and, mystified, studied Brasher before continuing.

"Furthermore, he gave me the practice outlines right up to the first game. As long as I'm in charge, we're going to follow them. Right now, the schedule calls for me to use the linemen on the charging machine and for you to work with the backs on blocking."

The two men's eyes locked and held. Brasher's swarthy face was flushed and marked by ill-concealed anger while Stewart's expression remained calm and clear. But once again, as it had been Saturday morning in the bleacher episode, it was Brasher who turned away.

But he didn't follow the practice outline. Not exactly, that is, for he introduced an entirely new blocking technique. Not that the block itself was new. But the way Brasher taught it, the way he used it, was entirely foreign to Henry Rockwell's clean, hard football blocking.

Brasher went through the block in slow motion and then described it. "Now, I call it a roll block or cut block. See, you throw your body past the defensive opponent. Naturally, the guy is hand fighting you, and when you go flying past him, he thinks he's been clever, see? So he drops his hands and looks for the ball carrier. And just then, your heels come flying around and up, and he gets it right in the stomach. And if you do it right, well, the opponent is through for the day—maybe longer!

"Now, we'll use that block on the reverse and on anything to the outside. We'll try it in slow motion first."

The Big Reds backs tried it in slow motion just the way Brasher had demonstrated, but the side glances they shot to one another spoke more clearly than words. Valley Falls's new backfield coach might teach them that kind of blocking, but that didn't mean they would use it. The Big Reds didn't play dirty football!

Chip was just coming downstairs, with Hoops trailing behind, when he heard footsteps on the front porch. It was Soapy. He'd started jogging each morning after Petey had put him on the scales.

"Hey, Chip, you see the paper this morning? Brasher's been appointed acting head coach!"

Chip picked up the paper from the porch, opening it to the sports section. "No!" he gasped. "Can't be! What about Chet?"

"Don't know," Soapy said, "but it's right here in Waters's column. Read it!"

Chip stared at Waters's column. He could scarcely believe his eyes.

TIMES AND SPORTS
By Muddy Waters

Good news for Valley Falls High School football fans. Reliable sources report that Thomas R. Brasher, new addition to the Big Reds coaching staff, will be appointed acting head coach of football beginning with the next practice.

A PASS AND A PRAYER

This is an excellent move and in line with Mayor Condon's school policy of bringing in new educational ideas and personalities.

Brasher is well fitted for the coaching assignment. He's an expert in modern football, a leader in excellent health, and is already extremely popular around town.

Coach Henry Rockwell has shown no improvement, and last reports indicate he may be hospitalized for several weeks. Many local fans probably don't know that the veteran coach is far past retirement regulations in both age and years of service. This illness probably signals the early retirement of the veteran coach. The *Times* wishes him well.

Chip pushed the paper into Soapy's hands and leaned back against the wall. "You suppose it's true, Soapy? You really think he's replaced Rock?"

"Got me, but I don't see how Waters could print it unless it's true."

Chip shook his head in disbelief. "Can't believe it. The Rock wouldn't do that to Chet."

"Maybe Zimmerman did it," Soapy suggested.

"Why?" Chip muttered. "Why in the world would he do that?"

Chip and Soapy weren't the only ones upset by the news. Most of the Big Reds saw the paper early that morning, and Chip's phone didn't stop ringing. Some of Chip's teammates were rebellious, even angry enough to drop out of football. Chip did his best to calm them down, advising them to wait until they got the whole story.

Pete Williams of the *Post* was more than upset. He called Zimmerman and, after learning the story was true, soundly rebuked the school administrator.

"What's going on up there?" Williams demanded. "How come the information wasn't released to the *Post* too? Or did you forget there are two papers in Valley Falls?"

Zimmerman was full of apologies. Then he made a mistake. He unwittingly explained he was merely following Condon's orders. That was enough for Williams! The *Post* was openly critical of Valley Falls's present administration, and Williams shared the feeling. When the *Post's* sports editor abruptly terminated the conversation by slamming the phone down, Mayor Condon and the high school principal had added more fuel to Pete Williams's dislike for their methods.

Chet Stewart could scarcely believe his eyes when he read the paper. He didn't waste time seeking confirmation. Ten minutes after he had opened the *Times* to the sports page, he was in Zimmerman's office.

The dejected principal waved wearily toward a chair. "Chet," he apologized, "I couldn't help it. I'm truly sorry. I *had* to do it."

"But why?" Stewart queried. "What about the Rock? Wasn't he consulted? I don't get it!"

"Neither do I, Chet. Please try to understand. You know the position I'm in. I have to follow orders, and Condon was dead set on this. There wasn't anything else I could do."

Stewart knew Zimmerman, all right. He knew him inside and out as Condon's puppet and a weak yes-man for the mayor's submissive school board. Stewart knew what he was up against. He rose slowly to his feet, completely deflated because of the unfair treatment he'd received. Chet knew this was a done deal, and now he had to protect his friend from hearing this devastating decision.

Zimmerman extended a restraining hand. "I hated to do this, Chet, but I'm just the principal. Everything will work out all right when Hank gets back. Do the best you can. And say, Chet, will you tell the squad at the start of practice this afternoon?"

Zimmerman breathed a deep sigh after Stewart closed the door and walked slowly down the hall. Rockwell's first assistant was a valuable member of the Valley Falls faculty, and the principal knew it well. The faculty liked the wiry little coach, and he was extremely popular with the athletes and the student body. Zimmerman breathed another deep sigh. He was sure glad *that* was over!

Zimmerman decided now was as good a time as any to inform Brasher of his new responsibility. He called the Physical Education office, and a few minutes later the new coach swaggered into the office. Zimmerman wasted few words on Brasher because there was something about the man he disliked and mistrusted. The harried principal told the blustering newcomer he was in charge of football during Rockwell's illness. As Zimmerman talked, he watched the heavy lips of Brasher's mouth form in a curve of self-satisfaction.

When the principal finished, Brasher turned around abruptly without a word. At the door, Zimmerman stopped him. "Brasher," he said softly, "Stewart said he'd tell the boys about the change at the start of practice this afternoon."

Brasher strode rapidly down the hall, his thoughts racing ahead of his heavy steps. At last he had the chance he deserved! "Now," he proclaimed, "I'll put that Stewart in his place, and that snotty Hilton kid will have to deal with me! And there'll be some coaching changes made too!"

CHAPTER 6

The Real Leader Emerges

POP BROWN, Valley Falls's veteran trainer, spent much of his time in the locker room. Maybe it was because he loved his work so much. Everything had to be just right where Pop was concerned. The immaculate floor and the neat arrangement of the room's equipment all attested to the trainer's insistence on cleanliness and order. Pop's cheerfulness and his fatherly tenderness toward everyone under his care gave the room an extra something.

But today something was plainly wrong. Chip sensed it as soon as he opened the door of his locker. Chip's teammates sensed it too. Something was missing. Not Pop, for he was bustling around just as every other day. No, this was something else, something pressing down on an athlete's heart and his feelings, making him tired of football and the rigorous training he hated and loved.

Chip figured it was Brasher. He'd seen Coach Stewart's grim face when the new, surly backfield coach came clattering down the iron steps leading from the office. Chip had quickly caught the venomous glint in Brasher's eyes as the bulky man from Illinois stood there on the bottom step.

It was different on the field too. There were no shouts of joy, no sudden warm-up sprints, no carefree race with a challenging teammate while waiting for the first whistle. No, today the Big Reds stood around in little groups, talking in subdued voices, each athlete aware he was waiting for the same thing and dreading the moment. Stewart's shrill whistle came at last, jarring them to move, and they trudged to the bleachers.

Chip led the way. A good captain was always out in front, always first to hit the blocking sled, to lead the team around the field. He sat down in the third row and quickly scanned Stewart's face. Then he caught his breath and pressed his back hard against the seat behind him, bracing himself for the shock. It was true.

Stewart cleared his throat, and words spilled out, one after another. "Guys," he began, "the coach is no better. They're not letting anyone in to see him now, but I talked to Mrs. Rockwell a while ago, and she said he's been asking about practice and seems worried about the progress the team's making. She also said she hopes everything will continue smoothly."

Chet paused. Chip knew his pause was to let the impact of his words sink in and also to get ready for the bad news to follow. Then Stewart was speaking again.

"Until the Rock gets back, Coach Brasher has been appointed acting head coach. He'll be in charge of the team."

Stewart gestured toward the boys in the bleachers. "Take charge, Brasher," he said evenly.

Brasher stood up, pulled up his football pants, stuck out his chest, and strutted over in front of the squad. He stood there quietly a moment while his eyes ranged from player to player until they reached Chip. Then, with his eyes boring straight into those of the Big Reds captain, he began to speak.

"This is as good a time as any to put everything on the line. Let's get it clear right now, I'm runnin' this team. Stewart will continue to work with the line, and I'll handle the backs just like before. But, beyond that, I expect to make some changes in the offense and maybe in the defense.

"First change will be in the offense, and we'll start this afternoon. Bring that board over here, Brown. This is gonna surprise most of you, but we're droppin' the *T*, as of now. We're puttin' in the single wing."

If Brasher's plan was to shock the Big Reds, he accomplished his purpose. Most of the team, stunned by Stewart's demotion, hadn't paid much attention to Brasher's first words. But this was different! What did he say? Did he really mean it? The Big Reds were experts in the use of Hank Rockwell's spin-T, had won the state championship with it just last year. They knew it by heart. Practically every regular turned his head and directed a bewildered glance toward Stewart for help. But Chet, sitting on the first row of the bleachers, was staring down at the ground, head bent low. Then the heads jerked around, and the boys looked to Chip for leadership.

But Chip was already on his feet. How he got there he didn't know, but there he was, and he was talking like lightning.

"Coach, I don't think you ought to change our system. We know the plays perfectly, and we've never been stopped. Coach Rockwell changed to the *T* just because it suited our personnel so well, and our first game is only ten days away."

Ugly veins bulged along Brasher's neck and rose to his temples. He stepped forward, pointing a shaking finger at the Big Reds captain.

"You mean the *T* is suited best for *you,* don't you, Hilton? Best so *you* can do all the ballhandling and grandstanding! Well, *you* can get it through your head right now that as long as I'm in charge of this team, *you* and everyone else will use any system I say! And I say it's the single wing! Another thing! When I want *your* advice, I'll ask for it. Now sit down and stay down!"

Chip didn't move. He just stood motionless, looking at the infuriated man. But that didn't mean he wasn't thinking.

His first reaction was a tremendous urge to tell Brasher he was through with football and then to leap over those two rows of bleachers and head for the locker room. But he knew every player in the stands would follow him, and he didn't want to be that kind of leader. Anyone could quit.

Then too there was the Rock to think about. Coach Rockwell wasn't in any condition to hear that his team had walked out while he was sick.

Brasher took another step forward. "I said sit down, Hilton!"

Chip locked stares with the incensed man for another moment, then reluctantly sat down. As he sank to his seat, a surge of thankfulness filled his heart at the spark of support he'd seen in his teammates' eyes as they waited for him to make his decision. Brasher probably never even realized how close he'd come to losing every Big Reds player and his head coaching assignment before he'd been in charge five minutes. If Chip Hilton had left the bleachers, every other player would have followed him off the field.

THE REAL LEADER EMERGES

Brasher waited, his hands on hips, his face contorted, until Chip sat down. Then he continued, "We went through the single wing yesterday before Stewart bothered us. We'll start it once more, this time for good. Oh, yes, we'll use the same signals. They'll work just the same since we're using a balanced line. As we go along, we'll get the special-play signals ironed out. Now, get out there and run the plays!"

The Big Reds ran through the plays, but their hearts weren't in the drills. Throughout practice, resentment mounted in their thoughts, which Brasher must have realized because he tried to buy them off with cheap praise and an easy workout. But when he dismissed them, purposefully omitting the usual "three laps and in," there were no joyous shouts or sudden dashes for the showers. The Big Reds were dejected, completely dejected.

In the showers and on their way home, the players talked it over. They knew one thing: Coach Rockwell had never approved the appointment of Brasher over Stewart, and they were certain he knew nothing about the change of offense. The Rock was sold on the *T*.

That evening it looked as if Chip was holding a practice session at the Sugar Bowl. First, Red Schwartz, Speed Morris, and Biggie Cohen appeared. Red, Soapy's caustic critic, spoke first.

"Look, Chip," Red said with emotion, "I don't have to play football. I could be working and helping out at home, and if it isn't going to be fun, I'm out of here. I guess I'll just drop out."

The three players with Red were just as determined, and it took all of Chip's persuasiveness to get them to promise to stick it out until Rock's condition improved.

A little later, the South-Siders arrived. Chris Badger, Cody Collins, Lou Mazotta, and Nick Trullo

were inseparable friends and stuck together in everything. They'd made up their minds not to play football
for Tom Brasher.

"He's no good, Chip," Cody warned, "and he's got it in
for you. I say we walk out! All of us! He can't make us
play football."

Again, Chip used all his resourcefulness to get his
four South-Side teammates to promise to stick it out.
Even then, Trullo made only a partial promise.

"I'll try to put up with it, Chip," Nick said gravely.
"But if it turns out the Rock isn't coming back, I'm turning in my uniform."

Ironically, about that same time, Tom Brasher, Jerry
Davis, and Muddy Waters were holding a celebration
dinner. They were in great spirits, and Brasher was reporting the day's events.

"You should've seen Stewart shrivel up," he gloated.
"And then the Hilton kid tried to play the big captain,
but I put him in his place, quick as," Brasher snapped his
fingers, "that!"

Waters was interested in material for his column.
"What about the new system, the single wing?" he asked.
"You going to put it in?"

"Absolutely!" Brasher declared triumphantly.
"Already started!"

"You sure you got the right material for the single
wing?" Davis asked doubtfully.

"Sure! Morris is the fastest one on the team. I'll use
him at left half. And that Badger kid, the one they call the
blockbuster, he's a powerful fullback. Collins is a solid
blocker, and I guess I'll have to use Hilton at quarter."

"I'd think Hilton would go better at left half," Waters
said thoughtfully. "You know Morris can't pass, and

much as we dislike Hilton, we've got to admit he can throw a football."

"That's right," Davis agreed, "and don't forget he can run. They say he's faster than Morris. Boots the ball a mile too. Fifty, sixty yards every time."

"Don't believe in passin'," Brasher growled. "Why take chances on interceptions or incompletions?"

"A running game is good, safe football," Waters warned, "but remember, Valley Falls fans are used to action."

"I'll give 'em action," Brasher promised, "real football action."

"The fans like Hilton," Davis said ruefully. "I wish we could get rid of him some way."

Brasher suddenly banged the table with his open hand, causing the dishes to jump and startling his two companions. "That's it!" he said excitedly. "Why didn't I think of it before? You remember that kid I was tellin' you about? Rankin? Tug Rankin?"

Davis nodded. "I remember," he said, "the one from Illinois. Sure, I remember. Why?"

"Because he's perfect for the quarterback spot. He'll make Hilton look like the nobody he really is. And he knows the single wing like he helped invent it! You s'pose Zimmerman would let him play?"

Davis laughed scornfully. "Hah," he chuckled, "Zimmerman will jump through a hoop and bark if Condon cracks the whip. Maybe this kid won't come."

"He'll come," Brasher said confidently. "The whole family will come if we can get his old man a job. Bet if I called the kid tonight, he'd be here tomorrow!"

Waters was cautious. "What about his eligibility?"

"Why wouldn't he be eligible?" Brasher demanded, glowering at the sportswriter. "There wouldn't be anything wrong if his family moved here, would there?"

"I don't know," Waters said defensively. "I just asked."

"Muddy's got something there, Tom," Davis cautioned. "After all, Rockwell wouldn't let other transfers play until they'd lived in town a year."

"Rockwell ain't runnin' things now," Brasher sneered in an ugly voice. "He's in the hospital, remember? I'm in charge, remember? If you're afraid to ask Condon, I'll do it myself. I know he'll do it!"

"Hold it, man," Davis said hastily. "Don't get all bent out of shape. We'll drive over to the mayor's house right now and see what he says. You guys wait in the car and let me handle Condon. Come on!"

Brasher was right. Mayor Condon was all for it, said he thought it might be a good idea. It was important to the entire community of Valley Falls to have good athletic teams, and he would go the limit to back any progressive program. He'd take care of the school part of it personally. Furthermore, he'd see that the boy's father got placed on the city payroll in some capacity. Davis had better move fast so the new player—what was his name, Rankin?—so Rankin could start school on the first day. Thursday, wasn't it? Yes, Brasher had better contact the Rankin family tonight.

Jerry Davis was elated! At last he had Rockwell down and nearly out. Now, to get the Rankin family a place to live. Good-bye Rockwell and good-bye Hilton!

CHAPTER 7

Football Candidates Wanted

THE PRINCIPAL of Valley Falls High School was thoroughly disgusted with his job and with himself. In most high schools, the principal, subject to the supervision of the superintendent of schools, directs the school's administration. But Zimmerman's hands were tied. He had been reduced to serving Mayor Condon's every wish and scheme. Politics had replaced solid educational foundations.

The Brasher episode had left Zimmerman so upset that every ring of the phone made him jump, adding more stress to his troubled mind. When the phone rang this Wednesday morning, he almost hoped it would be a complaining parent. He was wrong! It was Condon, and his oily voice put Zimmerman immediately on guard. The intimidated administrator thought, *What's he want this time?*

"Zim, how are you? This is Condon. I want you to write to New Paltz, Illinois, for the credits of a boy by the name of John Rankinowitz. The family is moving here this week, and I want the boy to enter school tomorrow. I believe he has completed his junior year, so the counselors have put him in the senior class. Tom Brasher will have him in your office tomorrow morning at nine o'clock."

Zimmerman breathed a sigh. This wasn't so bad. But Condon's next words ruined his temporary relief.

"I understand this young man is just the football player we need to retain our state championship, Zim, and I want you to see he gets all the help he needs. The community is counting on you."

Zimmerman drew a deep breath. Here it was again. Condon was forcing him once more to disregard regulations. Well, at least he could voice an objection.

"But he's a transfer, Mayor, and according to the rules of the State High School Athletic Association, a student who moves from one town to another can't participate until his family has established six months' residence."

Condon interrupted Zimmerman then, and his voice was cool and precise. "Coach Brasher brought a copy of the rules to my office, Zimmerman. The rule applies only to residents of the state. The Rankin family is moving here from Illinois."

"But Coach Rockwell has always insisted on observing the rule no matter where a student was from—"

"Zimmerman, I'm not interested in what Rockwell did. And I'm not interested in what he will think. The family will be here later this week, and I want the boy in school tomorrow with the rest of the seniors. And I want him to be eligible for football, understand?"

"I understand, Mayor," Zimmerman said worriedly, "and I suppose I'll have to do as you wish, but it seems to me we're avoiding the principle."

"We're doing no such thing! We're abiding by the letter of the law and by what is morally right. A family moves here in good faith, the head of the family has a job, and the student starts school on the first day. I see no moral or legal justification in prohibiting any student, under such circumstances, from enjoying every facility and activity that Valley Falls High School has to offer. But if you want to bring it up at the next school board meeting, I'll put you on the agenda.

"Further, Rockwell doesn't have the prerogative of making decisions in such cases. The boy is eligible, and I want no discussion about him with anyone. Good morning, Zimmerman."

The opening of school the next day was a welcome diversion from the team's football problems. For Chip, Speed Morris, Biggie Cohen, Red Schwartz, and Soapy Smith, it was the beginning of their last year at Valley Falls High School. Making good grades was important because they had set their hearts on entering the state university together the following year.

Chip was up early Thursday morning and, after opening up the Sugar Bowl, matched strides with Soapy as they headed for school. Just inside the main door, a crowd gathered in front of the huge bulletin board. The two friends shouldered their way close to the board and read the attention-getting poster.

FOOTBALL CANDIDATES WANTED
The football team needs a great number of additional players to inaugurate a two-platoon system of play. All candidates are welcome, regardless of experience. Report today for practice equipment.

TOM BRASHER
Acting Head Coach of Football

Soapy nudged Chip. "Two-platoon," he said sarcastically. "Maybe he plans to use the cheerleaders!"

A PASS AND A PRAYER

The first day of school was always exciting because of reunions with old friends, the usual vacation gossip, appraising new teachers, and comparing class schedules.

Chip was dressing for practice before he realized where the day had gone. As he dressed, he cast a measuring eye over Brasher's two-platoon candidates. The majority were inexperienced freshmen, but one candidate stood out from the rest. He was muscular, powerfully built, and seemed right at home in his uniform. Chip figured he and the newcomer were about the same age.

Biggie Cohen nodded toward the stranger and lifted one eyebrow in definite approval of his football possibilities. "Where'd he come from?"

Chip shook his head. "Never saw him before," he said softly. "Looks as if he knows what it's all about."

When the players reached the field, the new student quickly proved he did know what football was all about. Brasher led the way to the tackling dummy, and every time the new candidate tore into the canvas bag, he nearly broke it in half. That performance earned him the respect of every Big Reds veteran. But he kept to himself, making no effort to be friendly.

Chip spoke to the newcomer, welcoming him to the squad and offering to introduce the other veterans. But he remained aloof, simply saying he was glad to meet Chip and giving his name: "Tug. Tug Rankin."

Soapy was curious, and when something excited Soapy's curiosity, he never stopped until he had the answer. "You just move to town?" he asked, offering his friendliest smile.

Two little frown lines appeared between Rankin's brown eyes, and he deliberately looked Soapy up and down before replying. "Yeah," he said coolly. "So what?"

FOOTBALL CANDIDATES WANTED

Soapy's pleasant expression faded, and for a short moment he matched Rankin's challenging glare before turning abruptly away. Soapy was hurt—and irritated all the way through.

A little later, Brasher called for signal practice, and when the reserves lined up, Rankin was at quarterback. The regulars covertly watched the new guy; what they saw was a finished football player. Rankin had a wide face, high cheekbones, steely brown eyes set deep under heavy eyebrows, and a determined jawline. The wide, sloping shoulders, powerful arms with broad, square hands, and the heavy legs announced that here was an athlete—rugged, aggressive, and experienced.

Speed Morris's fastback Mustang was crammed with members of the Hilton A. C. on the way home, and everybody was talking about the new guy, Rankin.

"There," Chip said decisively, "is a football player!"

"Could tell that soon as he walked out on the field," Speed added.

"Sticks out all over the guy," Biggie agreed, "just like Soapy's ice cream paunch!"

Soapy sucked in his stomach and expanded his chest. "Look at that," he growled, pounding his chest. "Rock! Hard as a rock!"

Red Schwartz murmured something about Soapy's head and a rock, then swung the conversation back to Rankin. "You know something," Red said speculatively, "I got a hunch Brasher knows the guy. I think he's a ringer!"

"A ringer? You mean an impostor?" Chip repeated. "No, you're wrong there, Red. Zimmerman wouldn't allow that."

"No?" Schwartz said doubtfully. "Well, that guy has played a lot of football, and if he's played it in another high school, then he isn't eligible at Valley Falls for a year. And, if this guy hasn't been playin' high school ball, he's been playin' somewhere, and that's even worse. I say he's a ringer!"

"I go along with that," Speed said. "He's a ringer! Wait and see!"

Biggie summed it up. "Anyway, he looks as though he knows his way around on a football field, and his eligibility is the school's business, and it isn't any of ours, yet. If Brasher's gonna use the two-platoon system, we can sure use the guy." He paused, then added, "How's the Rock? Anyone hear?"

"Chet said there wasn't any change," Chip said somberly. "Guess they still don't know exactly what's wrong with him."

"I sure wish he'd hurry up and get back," Morris said gloomily. "He'd put Brasher in his place fast!"

Cohen shifted his weight over against Soapy, bringing a sharp protest. "Don't worry," the big tackle drawled, "Brasher will trip over his own feet, one way or another."

While Speed's red fastback raced along with its noisy occupants, Jerry Davis and Tom Brasher were cruising away from Ohlsen Field in the Davis Cadillac.

"You get Rankin's old man a job?" Brasher asked.

"Sure did!" Davis boasted. "The mayor created a special position for him, sort of an unofficial investigator. He's not allowed to do real detective work, just investigate things the mayor wants checked out. How's the kid?"

Brasher grunted. "How is he? He's great, that's how he is. Wait till you see him! He's dynamite! About two hundred, five-eleven, hard as steel, and tough as they come."

"Better be tough if he's going to beat out Hilton. Hilton's good, Tom; don't underrate the guy. And he's tough too. I heard he had to defend someone and whipped a couple of the toughest guys in this town."

"Don't make me laugh, Jerry," Brasher retorted. "Rankin could take him with one hand."

"Maybe," Davis said dryly. "You got a story for Muddy? I'm meeting him at six-thirty."

"Yeah, I got a story—a good one. I want him to play up this two-platoon system I'm s'posed to be puttin' in—"

"Supposed to be putting in!" Davis repeated incredulously. "You told me and Muddy you're going to use it for sure. What happened?"

"Aw, I was just puttin' on an act. I'm only usin' that two-platoon stuff to get Hilton off the first string."

"Don't get it."

"You will when you see the scrimmage on Saturday."

Davis was worried. "Hey, you gotta be careful. A lot of people are already talking about that two-platoon stuff. Don't start vacillating!"

"Look, Jerry," Brasher said patiently, "we ain't got more'n twelve, thirteen football players. I know that. I'm just usin' this platoon idea to shift Hilton to the second string and give the people a chance to see Tug in action. Get it?"

Davis got it and there was real admiration in the look he gave Brasher. He involuntarily pressed his foot down hard on the accelerator. He couldn't wait to let Waters in on Brasher's masterful strategy.

On the sports page of Friday's *Times* was a story about Brasher's two-platoon system and an announcement of a special intrasquad scrimmage scheduled for Saturday afternoon. But it was the two-platoon system that drew the most comment. Waters had really endorsed Brasher's new plans in his column.

A PASS AND A PRAYER

Soapy Smith and Petey Jackson were working at the fountain early that Friday morning, and Soapy was reading Waters's column.

"Listen to this, Petey," Soapy said sarcastically. "'Outmoded *T*'! 'Two-platoon'! Baloney! Here, read it!"

> Tom Brasher, Valley Falls's new acting head football coach, has brought innovative, big-time football contributions to the Big Reds. Coach Brasher has added the famed Tigers' single-wing formation to the team's outmoded *T*, and the state champions are now equipped with an attack that can meet any type of defense.
>
> In addition, the popular newcomer plans the installation of the two-platoon system, which will reduce fatigue, give more athletes a chance to play, practically eliminate injuries, and give the fans more action.
>
> Big Reds fans are invited to attend the two o'clock Saturday afternoon scrimmage when Coach Brasher's two-platoon system will be on display for the first time.
>
> Admission is free, and the popular coach promises to unveil several new players destined to make Big Reds football history.

"I see what you mean," Petey said gravely. He glanced at the clock. "Hey, you guys better beat it. You only got ten minutes to get to school. Hey, Chip, it's time to go!"

Chip hurried out of the storeroom, pulling on his jacket and joining Soapy at the door. As the two boys hustled up Main Street, Soapy told Chip about the article.

"You think the guy really means it, Chip? You think he'll *really* use the platoon?"

FOOTBALL CANDIDATES WANTED

Chip shook his head ruefully. "Don't know, Soapy. Most coaches who use the platoon system have an offensive team that runs the ball and a defensive team they send in when the opponents have the ball. Man, we haven't got enough players for anything like that. We don't even have a single sub with any real football experience."

"There sure weren't any new players out there yesterday," Soapy declared, "except for that Rankin guy. I don't like his attitude, Chip, but I think he's a football player."

That afternoon Tom Brasher made his first move toward the establishment of his two-platoon system, and it troubled the Big Reds regulars. After reviewing the single wing, Brasher turned his back on the players and wrote two lists of names on the board. Then he turned back to scan the shocked faces of the Big Reds, smirking with self-satisfaction at the effect of his action.

"Until further notice," Brasher announced harshly, "these two platoons will work as units."

He paused, his cold eyes glittering with malice and his tongue licking his lips in obvious pleasure. He enjoyed this moment!

Chip's eyes ran up and down the lists of names in disbelief. Then he quickly glanced at Chet Stewart. Stewart wasn't even looking at the board, so Chip checked the lists once more. This wasn't possible. He wasn't on the first team, and neither was Soapy.

A PASS AND A PRAYER

TEAM 1		TEAM 2
Peck	l.e.	Smith
Cohen	l.t.	Knox
Rice	l.g.	Ferris
Trullo	c.	Davis
DeWitt	r.g.	Blaine
Schwartz	r.e.	Hill
Rankin	q.b.	Hilton
Morris	l.h.	Taylor
Badger	f.b.	Carroll
Collins	r.h.	Harding

There was dead silence. Then a murmur started, which grew almost tumultuous before Brasher raised his hands and shouted for quiet. Almost every Big Reds regular turned his head toward Chip, waiting for him to make a move. But Chip shook his head, and one by one, they turned back to study the board.

"Quiet!" Brasher ordered. "I said quiet! Now pay attention. We're gonna have a scrimmage at two o'clock tomorrow afternoon, and that's the way *you'll* line up. We don't have any men for substitutions and each team will have to play the whole game. Both squads will use the same offense and the same defense.

"Naturally, when we open our schedule, we'll use one team for offense and the other for defense. Now get out there and run some plays."

It was the longest football practice Chip had ever endured. He did his best and worked hard with his inexperienced teammates, but it was a discouraging task. There was no timing in the backfield, no precision in the movement of the line, and almost every play resulted in a fumble. Chet Stewart, following along behind Chip's team, worked patiently on the unfamiliar single-wing plays, but he was obviously disheartened.

Soapy's constant muttering was no help either. The glib joker was openly rebellious, and his antagonistic tirade against Brasher could be heard all over the field. For the first time that Chip could remember, Soapy was unresponsive to his pleas for silence.

Chip couldn't blame Soapy. The incorrigible comic was a fine football player, one of the best ends in the state, and a two-year regular. Soapy might joke and cut up between classes and around the Sugar Bowl, but on the field he was a serious, dedicated athlete.

Chip figured Brasher must have sensed that Soapy disliked him and was giving the two of them the same treatment. Well, Chip Hilton had been in tough spots before, and he wasn't going to kowtow to a man like Brasher, even if it meant he never played football again.

CHAPTER 8

Confrontations and Conversations

SPEED MORRIS was in a hurry going home. The heavy-throated gurgling of the red Mustang pulling away from the parking lot was a lonely sound. Chip also wanted to get away from Ohlsen Field as fast as possible, and he didn't want to talk. His friends felt the same way. Only a grumpy good night was muttered as each unloaded in front of his house.

Chip hurried through dinner and then drove to see Chet Stewart. He had to straighten out a few things. Stewart was at home and welcomed Chip, yet Stewart was unsure of how to begin as they sat down on the porch. He didn't get a chance to begin; Chip got right to the point.

"Coach, I don't think the guys can take this much longer. I know I can't. What's been going on?"

Stewart took his time before trying to answer, rubbing his hand nervously through his thinning hair and studying the arm of his chair. After what seemed minutes to

Chip, Stewart started to talk, and then suddenly all his frustration spilled out in a steady stream of words.

"Chip, this is a difficult time. The Rock's worse. Going through a crisis. Doc says if anything upsets him right now, it might mean he won't come through it. I know what you guys are up against. But I'm taking it and I'm going to keep on until the Rock gets back. You can be sure Tom Brasher and a few other people in this town are in for some real trouble before this nonsense is finished.

"Mrs. Rockwell and Doc Jones have kept all this football mess away from Rock. They've been telling him everything is fine. Doc doesn't even let him see a paper. But you know as well as I do, if the players walk out, quit football, the Rock will know about it within an hour. No, Chipper, we've got to stick it out, and you're the only person who can keep the team together. You've got to do that, no matter what. There's more going on here than football. You've got to keep them from talking about giving up. This won't last forever. We can beat it, if we stick together."

Chip Hilton didn't know how to quit, and Chet's talk had been just what he needed. He was his old self again. He dropped off the car at home and a few minutes later walked into the Sugar Bowl and smack into trouble.

Petey Jackson's doleful expression was warning enough, and his words confirmed Chip's fears. Petey gestured toward the storeroom. "The whole team's back there, Chip, and they're quittin' football. Mr. Schroeder's talkin' to 'em now. You better hurry back there! They ain't foolin'!"

John Schroeder owned the Sugar Bowl and the drugstore adjoining it. He was one of Valley Falls's most stable and respected citizens and an enthusiastic sports fan. He and Doc Jones, the town's "old reliable," were inseparable companions who enthusiastically backed Big Reds athletics. A close friend to Big Chip Hilton before the great athlete's untimely death, John Schroeder had taken a fatherly interest in Little Chip, giving him a job at the Sugar Bowl and encouraging his sports and college ambitions. Indeed, John Schroeder was a good friend.

Petey Jackson had caught the first onslaught of the determined Big Reds regulars; they had left no doubt in his mind that they were finished with football. They were coming to tell Chip and had run into John Schroeder, who invited them into the storeroom to wait for Chip.

Schroeder knew something serious was going on. But he was too smart to hurry them, too smart to question them when he could clearly see from their tight-lipped expressions they weren't ready to talk with anyone except Chip. So he talked about Rockwell and school and everything except football. That's the way Chip found them when he opened the door and eased into the room.

Schroeder was glad to turn the situation over to Chip. "Excuse me, boys," he said gently, "I've got to speak with Doc Jones. See you later."

Seconds after the door closed, the dam broke. "We're through, Chip," Biggie Cohen said flatly, "as of right now."

"That's right," Chris Badger added, "we're playing no more football for Valley Falls while that guy's in charge."

Murmurs of support followed the husky fullback's words, and Chip looked around while he collected his thoughts. They were all there, just as Petey had said, all Rock's regulars. The South-Siders—Badger, Trullo, Mazotta, and Collins—were standing side by side along one wall. Directly opposite them, the West-Siders were lined up, just the way it used to be when these two groups had been bitter enemies. Chip's eyes quickly swept over them. Biggie Cohen—bulky, dominant, and determined—was in the center, flanked by Schwartz, Morris, and Smith on one side, and by Rice and Peck on the other.

"He's breaking up the team, Chip," Morris said firmly, "and it doesn't make sense."

"That's right," Cody Collins said belligerently, "and if no one else is gonna do something about it, we are!"

"He's just dividing the team for his phony scrimmage," big Nick Trullo said sarcastically.

Chip tried to reason with them, telling them how vital it was to the Rock for them to keep playing and trying to explain that the new offense would give the backs a better break and be better for Speed and Cody and Chris.

"You know as well as I do," Chip said, "Rock built the offense around my ability to pass and kick. What if I got sick?"

But the Big Reds weren't having any of that. Their voices rose in a tumult of protests and arguments.

"Who wants a break?" Collins demanded. "Me, I don't want to carry the ball! I like to block!"

"Sick!" someone said, disgusted. "Look at the guy! Never been sick in his life!"

"What do we need a new offense for?" another voice shrilled. "Who stopped us last year?"

"Yeah, and who's gonna stop us this year?" someone else asked. "Who's gonna stop the *T* the way we know it?"

"Brasher!" Schwartz said heatedly. "Tom Brasher. He and his pet ringer, that's who!"

Chip held up his hands for silence. When they were quiet, he laid it on the line, directing his words chiefly at Biggie Cohen and Chris Badger, looking the two leaders straight in the eyes. He asked them as personal friends and teammates to stick it out for just one more week.

"Look, guys," he said emotionally, "Brasher is coming down on me mostly. I'm the one getting most of the grief, along with Soapy and Chet Stewart. But we can take it. And we will take it if you go along with us and help us.

A PASS AND A PRAYER

If you walk out now, the Rock will know it before any of us get home. Honest!

"Chet told me the Rock doesn't know anything is wrong. Doc Jones doesn't let him read the papers and said he isn't going to until he lets him out of the hospital.

"So far as the single wing is concerned, we can use any formation. With the material we've got, we don't even need a formation. And this new guy, Rankin, may be OK. Let's give him a chance. The fact that Brasher's using him at quarterback doesn't worry me. Remember, it's the team that counts!"

Chip talked for half an hour, and when he finished, he had the halfhearted consent of his teammates to keep going a little longer. But they didn't look too happy as they filed out of the storeroom, and they didn't hang around the Sugar Bowl very long afterward. They were still disgruntled, and they had company.

Chet Stewart hadn't touched his dinner. He was so worried about the division of the team that he couldn't stand it any longer. He had to talk with Brasher tonight. This had gone far enough. If only the Rock wasn't so sick.

Stewart had no trouble finding Brasher. The new coach was sitting outside the *Times* office in Jerry Davis's car.

"Got a minute, Brasher?" Stewart said coolly. "Could I speak to you privately?"

Brasher gestured toward Davis. "Jerry's my friend, Stewart," he said insolently. "Anything you've got to say to me, you can say in front of him."

"Well," Stewart said bluntly, "I want to know if you intend to continue with this two-platoon foolishness and riding Chip Hilton?"

Brasher grinned. "Oh, the grandstander's been cryin' on your shoulder, has he? Now isn't that too bad! Your little show-off boy can't take it."

CONFRONTATIONS AND CONVERSATIONS

"That's not true, Brasher," Stewart said in a cold, level tone. "Hilton isn't like that. I'm talking about your obvious dislike for one of the best athletes we've ever had in this town and about the unfair advantage you're taking of him. You know as well as I do we don't have enough players for two teams. You're using this two-platoon nonsense to cover up your vindictive plan to shove Hilton off the first team."

That barrage hurt Brasher, but he controlled himself with a violent effort. "I oughta teach you a big lesson," he said angrily, grasping the handle of the door.

Jerry Davis placed a hand on Brasher's arm. "Take it easy, Tom," he warned. "Take it easy."

Stewart hadn't moved and had watched Brasher's show of anger impassively. He hadn't backed up and he hadn't shown any alarm. When he spoke, his voice was still calm and quiet.

"Another thing, Brasher," he said coolly, "this new quarterback you've imported looks a little too old and a little too experienced not to have played a lot of ball. If you're trying to pull a fast one, I advise you to be careful. Rockwell won't stand for ringers!"

"Then he'll just have to take it layin' down! Just like he is now," Brasher snarled.

For the first time, Stewart's face showed emotion. He felt the blood rush hot and angry to his face. He strained to control his impulse to lash out at Brasher.

"Who's running the team anyway?" Davis interposed. "You or Tom?"

Stewart ignored Davis completely, but the interruption helped him regain control. He realized further discussion with Brasher could only lead to a fight, and that would mean trouble for the Rock and for the team. Without another word, he turned and walked away.

Stewart took a long walk. After an hour he had

regained his composure and, on his way home, stopped to have a talk with Louise Rockwell.

No, there wasn't any change in Henry's condition, but sick as he was, he kept asking about the team. He always worried about the boys, sick or well, and he seemed particularly concerned right now. He seemed to worry most of all about the new coach, just as if he sensed there was some kind of trouble at the school.

Of course, he knew nothing specific because Doc Jones had outlawed football talk and had permitted no visitors. But Henry had always been able to smell out trouble, and now he felt something wasn't right with the team. Louise Rockwell would be glad when her husband was well enough for Chet to visit. Chet could reassure him.

"Chet," Mrs. Rockwell said just before Stewart left, "I've been reading the papers, and I know just what you've been going through. I want you to know how much I appreciate your patience. And, Chet, please tell Chip I said for him, especially, to keep his chin up. Tell him everything will work out all right. Hank's pretty ill right now, and anything that would excite him might be dangerous. I want you and Chip both to know how thankful I am you're his friends. Please keep him in your prayers."

After leaving Mrs. Rockwell, Stewart continued walking until he came to 131 Beech Street, the Hilton home. The only one home was Hoops, napping in his favorite chair on the porch.

Chet Stewart sat there for a long time before he heard Chip's quick steps on the sidewalk. The long, whispered fellowship that followed seemed to lift their spirits. Chet whistled a little on his way home, and Chip even picked his mother up and swung her around in his usual cheery manner when he said good night.

CHAPTER 9

Benched without a Chance

VALLEY FALLS was a football town, and long before two o'clock the sidelines in Ohlsen Stadium were jammed. Brasher was really putting on a display, hiring extra officials, suiting up the two squads in different colored uniforms and placing them on opposite sides of the field. Chet Stewart was in charge of Chip's team, and Brasher, of course, supervised the first string. The fans liked the show!

Jerry Davis had strategically positioned his friends on both sides of the field with specific instructions to "sell" Brasher, Tug Rankin, and the single wing. They did a good job, initiating the cheers and stirring up sideline remarks.

"This is a *great* idea!"

"Yeah, wonder why Rockwell never did it like this?"

"What's this two-platoon stuff all about?"

"Oh, nothing especially new, except here in Valley Falls. College and university teams use it. One team for offense and one for defense."

"The one with Hilton must be the offensive team."

A PASS AND A PRAYER

"Don't think so. Badger, Collins, and Morris are over there with the new coach. The regular line's over there too."

Within the crowd, not everyone agreed with the planted supporters. They were fans who remembered Rockwell's great teams and especially last year's undefeated state champions.

"Don't get it! Hilton's the best passer in the state. Good runner too! If he isn't good enough for this Brasher's offense, it must really be something."

"We'll see! Every coach in the state put Hilton on the first team. Averaged forty-eight yards last year in punting, and that's as good as many college kickers in the country. Didn't miss an extra point either!"

"This new coach, Brasher, sure has some good ideas."

"Seems pretty smart, too, changing to the single wing. Every coach in the league was gettin' wise to Rockwell's *T*."

"Then why didn't they stop it last year if they knew so much about it?" a disgusted voice observed. "Yeah, right!"

Out on the field, Chip began spiraling long, booming punts far down the field, and the spectators' interest shifted. Every time Chip put his foot to the ball, the crowd cheered. Davis's fans couldn't compete with the crowd's admiration for Chip's kicking.

Chet Stewart was thrilled! He had purposefully sent Chip out to display his kicking. It was all a part of the plan he and Chip had worked out the night before.

Brasher didn't like the cheers and the attention Chip's punting drew, so he signaled the officials to start the scrimmage. The referee's blast sent the two squads circling Brasher and Stewart, and Chet motioned for Chip to go out for the toss. Stewart knelt in the center of the nervous reserves, and each player's face was set with determination. Chip Hilton was their leader, and they were just as upset about the Rankin deal as the Big Reds first team. But they didn't let their emotions interfere with Coach Stewart's directions.

Chip trotted out to the middle of the field—the captain of the reserves but captain in the heart of every player in a Big Reds uniform, Brasher or no Brasher. Biggie Cohen waited with the officials, his eyes conveying words the referee didn't notice and wouldn't have understood anyway. The referee tossed the coin, and Chip called, "Tails!" Tails it landed, and Chip chose to kick.

While Chip was out on the field, Stewart talked bluntly to the little circle of reserves. "OK, guys," he said, "this is it! We're outweighed and facing the best team in the state. But I believe we've got something extra to fight for. Pay attention to Chip. Listen to him all the time. On the defense, I want the line to dig in, charge low, and let the backs make the tackles. Remember, they haven't got a passer, so we can all converge on the ball carrier. Here comes Chip now, guys. Let's give him all we've got!"

Chip leaned over and thrust both arms into the tangled mass of hands and then led the way out to the forty-yard line. He didn't hear the supporting cries of his team or spot the absence of enthusiasm in Brasher's squad. But he did note the five-three-three receiving formation with Rankin anchored in the middle of the last threesome, right where Chip Hilton always lined up, on the ten-yard line.

Chip grinned as he leaned over the ball. Rankin was not going to run this one back! He hefted the ball for a second and placed it carefully on the kicking tee. Then he backtracked his usual seven strides and raised his arms.

The referee's whistle started him forward, and Chip smacked the ball squarely. He kept his head down and followed through as far as he could with his long right leg. He knew he'd tagged that one; it was into the end zone, far over Rankin's head, and out of bounds.

It was first down on the twenty. When the regulars broke from their huddle, they faced an eight-man line with Chip about ten yards back, flanked by Taylor and Harding. Stewart planned the eight-man line to halt Brasher's running attack. The regulars were held to a single yard, when Rankin sent Morris on a smash over tackle Lou Mazotta. The next time they came out of the huddle, they faced a six-three-two defense, also part of Chet and Chip's game plan. Chip was instructed to change the defense on every play, choosing a formation that concentrated its strength against the run and risking a pass.

Rankin next tried Cody Collins on a reverse around left end, and he was smothered for no gain by Jarrod "Hillie" Hill, Ken Morton, and Dan Harding. Tug's face was worried when the defense shifted to the left on the next play. Chip figured it right. Rankin was gambling on Speed Morris on a reverse around the right side. So Chip called sharply to Soapy and motioned Jordan "Air" Taylor to shift farther to the left. It worked. Speed came dashing around Red Schwartz's end like lightning, but there were too many reserves waiting for him, all diving under the massed defense. It was Chip who made the tackle, and he sent Speed flying back, losing two yards, with a straight shoulder tackle that jarred them both.

But they got up grinning. Chip pulled his best friend to his feet, and Speed slapped Chip affectionately on the back. That set off the fireworks. Tug Rankin's face was livid. He smashed his helmet to the ground and turned on Morris.

"What is this?" Rankin raged. "The prom? We playin' football or you guys going steady? You lost two yards on that play, you quitter!"

BENCHED WITHOUT A CHANCE

Speed didn't say a word, just grabbed Rankin's jersey in both hands and drove him back on his heels. No one called Speed Morris a quitter and got away with it. But that was as far as the confrontation went. Players rushed between them, pulling the two angry players apart. Brasher and Stewart came running across the field, shouting, waving their arms, and rushing into the middle.

Brasher had been raving on the sidelines, feeding his own anger. The reserves had stopped his regulars cold, and he took it out on Morris. That was a mistake. The all-state halfback was popular with his teammates, and only Chip's and Coach Stewart's presence prevented a spontaneous team walkout.

Davis's cohorts tried unsuccessfully to focus criticism on the flashy speedster. But Speed Morris was popular with everyone. He'd been Henry Rockwell's breakaway runner for three years, and the fans liked him. But Davis's supporters also tried to overlook Rankin's aggressiveness toward Morris.

The referee added to the Big Reds' misery by stepping off five yards for delaying the game, and that put the ball back on the fourteen, fourth down and sixteen. Chip hustled back to the forty, chuckling to himself. Imagine the second team holding the Big Reds regulars. Now to run this punt back for a score. It probably would be the only chance the reserves would have unless they clicked with a pass. Chip had never seen Rankin kick, but he knew about the rest of them. Speed could kick a little but was never good for more than forty yards.

The regulars came out of their huddle; Morris was in the kicking slot. "So Rankin can't kick," Chip murmured. "Good!" Speed's kick was short and low, and Chip took it on the thirty-five at full speed. James "J. P." Peck, in Soapy's place at left end for the regulars, got off to a slow start. So Chip cut toward J. P. and the right sideline. Then he saw Cohen. Biggie, from his position at left tackle, was always the first lineman down the field under punts, and he was hunting down Chip.

Chip knew feints wouldn't work on Biggie, so he headed straight at the big tackle. At the last split second, he pivoted and spun away from Cohen's grasp. He eluded the driving shoulders, but one of Biggie's heavy arms swept Chip's foot out from under his body, and he whirled through the air like a gymnast, his feet and free arm clawing as he tried desperately to regain his footing. Just when it seemed as if he was going to go down, he jackknifed his legs and regained his balance, but the momentum propelled him into more trouble. Speed and J. P. both dove for him at the same time and that helped; they met in the air, and Chip was free.

Free, except for Tug Rankin. The husky quarterback was roaring across the five-yard line, bitterness gleaming in his eyes. Chip never changed his course as he headed for the goal line, welcoming this first opportunity to meet Rankin head-on. The crash of their impact could be heard all over the field, but it was Chip who won, who drove through Rankin and over those last five yards for the touchdown.

Rankin got up, shaking his head, but the shock hadn't knocked the hate out of his eyes. Chip didn't notice and wouldn't have thought much about it even if he had. But Chip's teammates saw it, and they didn't like it.

Seconds later, with Taylor holding the ball, Chip kicked the extra point and the reserves led 7-0. But that was it. Power, weight, and experience began to show. After Chip booted the second kickoff over the end line for a touchback, the regulars drove steadily down the field. Not that the reserves didn't fight. Their determination and spirit were contagious, and the stands swung solidly behind them. But it wasn't enough. Brasher's single-wing regulars defeated the Valley Falls second team, 18-7.

Chip had played brilliantly, evening up much of the regulars' ground gains with his long, accurate out-of-bounds punts. He'd demonstrated that football is a multidimensional sport, requiring more than a running game for a successful team.

In spite of Davis's efforts to create enthusiasm for Brasher's single wing, Tug Rankin, and the two-platoon system, many Big Reds fans left Ohlsen Stadium far from convinced they'd seen a championship team in action.

Tom Brasher tramped savagely off the field and barged into the varsity locker room and up the iron steps without a word. Chet Stewart followed, pausing for a moment to check for possible injuries.

"Nice going, you guys," he said softly, his warm eyes moving from player to player. "That was a good workout. See you Monday."

A little later, Brasher hurried down the side steps of the gym and joined Davis and Muddy Waters, who were waiting in Jerry's car. Brasher slid in beside them without a word.

"We didn't do so good," Davis said ruefully.

"They weren't putting out," Brasher snapped. "Anyone could see that!"

"Hilton was putting out," Waters said sourly. "He's the best high school football player I ever saw, and believe me, it breaks my heart to say it."

"You better use him, Tom," Davis advised.

Brasher shook his head stubbornly. "Rankin's my quarterback," he said in a surly voice. "Tug didn't have a chance today. Give the kid time."

"I was listening to the crowd," Waters said reflectively, "and I think it's a mistake to shelve Hilton. The fans want him, and he's the only kid you've got who can kick, pass, and run."

"Don't have to use passes," Brasher growled.

"Well," Waters warned, "there comes a time in every game and to every team when some kind of kick is important. Don't overlook that Hilton punts, kicks the extra point, and place-kicks from any spot inside the thirty. With the goal post on the end line, that's a forty-yard boot. Lots of coaches would give their right arm for that kind of kicker."

"Another thing, Tom," Davis added, "it's important to win. Keep in mind the Hilton kid is secondary. Our first and most important objective is getting rid of Rockwell."

"I hate that kid's guts," Brasher grated. "I'm gonna get him some way if it's the last thing I ever do."

"Thought you said Rankin was going to do that," Waters murmured. "Seems to me it worked out the other way around."

Brasher lapsed into a sullen silence. When they were parting for the night, Davis again tried to impress Brasher with the importance of winning.

"You see, Tom," he explained patiently, "we've got to sell you too. We can, if you give the fans a winner. Muddy's doing his part in the paper, and I'm doing a lot of talking around town, but everything depends on you putting out a winning team."

"Right!" Waters added, "and if it comes down to winning or losing, use Hilton. Don't bite off your nose to spite your face."

"I don't need Hilton to win," Brasher said confidently. "You wait and see."

"There's one more angle we've got to cover and cover

fast, Tom," Davis said. "The school paper, the *Yellow Jacket*. You've got to get on the good side of that Orlander kid. We've got to get the school kids on your side. They carry a lot of weight. You work on Orlander, OK?"

Brasher continued to use Rankin with the regulars and Chip with the reserves. On Tuesday in a squad race, Chip quickly proved he was the fastest player on the field. He led all the way, finishing ten yards ahead of Speed Morris, who came in second. Chip noted with grim satisfaction that Rankin ended up far back in the pack.

The Wednesday scrimmage consisted of a series of slow-motion rehearsals of each of the single-wing plays and then a full-speed drive with live blocking and tackling. Chip played in the safety position, but he and Soapy made most of the tackles. The first team had gained complete domination over the reserves by this time, and the contact work seemed hardly worthwhile. Chip had to admit Rankin could block. Brasher's quarterback in the single wing was used chiefly for that chore, and Tug Rankin proved he was expert in that phase of football.

Brasher spoke directly to Chip only once that week and then it was to praise Rankin's work at quarterback. "Watch how Rankin uses a cross-body block to drive the defensive end out of the off-tackle play, Hilton," he said sharply. "Tug takes care of the end all by himself, and that means I can use the extra blocker on a defensive back."

Brasher turned to Rankin. "Now run an in-and-out sweep, slow motion, Tug, and show us how to get rid of a tough tackle. Watch this, Hilton! Watch Tug take care of the tackle! When you hit 'em that way, they carry 'em off the field, and that's what we want!"

Brasher then wheeled abruptly away from Chip, leaving the Big Reds captain standing there with burning cheeks. Tug Rankin, chuckling just loud enough for Chip to hear him, then led the regulars through another play.

The regulars muttered to themselves, but they remembered their promise and their sympathetic eyes followed Chip as he turned and walked back to the reserves.

It took all of Chip's positive outlook to keep from dwelling on Brasher's handling of the team, but he found the answer in studying and working. Before he knew it, Friday had rolled around. Then he received another blow. This one hurt most of all. For it was played up in the *Yellow Jacket* and by Jiggs Orlander, of all people! But there it was for every student to see.

ON THE SIDELINES
By Jiggs Orlander

Tomorrow's the day! The Big Reds open with Salem at Ohlsen Stadium! New season, new coach, new style of play, new quarterback! Yes, Captain Chip Hilton, all-state quarterback, benched for newcomer Tug Rankin! Reason? Rankin experienced in single-wing blocking technique! Hilton to be used with reserves in two-platoon system and for kicking!

Coach Brasher is optimistic! Promises strong running attack! New system is ideal for Big Reds running back Speed Morris!

Two o'clock! Come early! Sellout assured! Valley Falls's 100-piece marching band at 1:15!

Sections D, E, and F reserved for students on 50-yard line! Bring your student card and start the state champs off right! See you there! Go Big Reds!

Chip groaned and thrust the paper into his backpack. Benched! All-state quarterback and team captain, benched without a chance!

CHAPTER 10

Turn in Your Uniform

SALEM LOOKED good in the pregame warm-up, charging three teams up and down the field and then going into group work. Salem's kicking was good, too, and the Big Reds began to get the jitters. Chip wasn't jittery, but he was fighting a dull ache in his heart and the bitter knowledge that he'd been benched. His feelings affected his kicking. The edge was gone. He didn't know whether Brasher would send him out for the toss, even though he was still captain.

But when the officials bunched in the center of the field, Brasher sent Chip out with instructions to choose to kick if he got the chance. Salem's captain won the toss and elected to defend the south goal. Chip followed orders and said Valley Falls would kick. He brought the news back to Brasher. Chip sat down on the bench, looking at his feet and trying to fight down the choking feeling creeping higher and higher until he felt his throat would burst.

A PASS AND A PRAYER

Chip was so deep in thought Brasher had to call him three times before it registered, and he glanced up to find his teammates waiting for him. Then he caught the words and grabbed his helmet, almost knocking Soapy off the bench as he sprang to his feet and joined the circle.

"You kick off, Hilton," Brasher said coldly, "right over the goal, if you can."

Chip experienced such a surge of power he felt as though he could have kicked the ball out of the stadium. He nearly did it seconds later, sending the ball into the end zone on the fly and into the south stands on the first bounce. Chip charged down the field, expertly dodging blockers, knowing it was unnecessary but still motivated by the thrill of starting the game.

Then, waiting for the referee to put the ball in play on the twenty, Chip saw Rankin spring up from the bench and sprint directly toward him. His heart sank. He never saw Tug's contemptuous thumb gesture toward the sidelines, never saw the bitter faces of his teammates when they realized the significance of the substitution. He never saw much of the first quarter or knew who scored the first Big Reds touchdown following the initial march down the field.

But he jumped to his feet and ran out on the field with joyous strides when Brasher sent him in for Rankin to kick the extra point. Speed Morris took Nick Trullo's perfect snap and plunked the ball down on the turf just before Chip drove into it sending it over the center of the crossbar.

This time, Chip's kickoff was taken in at the goal line, and the Salem ball carrier got back to the thirty before he was downed. After the tackle, Chip didn't wait for Rankin to take his place; he just pivoted and headed back for the bench on the double without giving Rankin a glance.

Soapy Smith handed Chip his jacket, and the two

buddies braced shoulders as they watched the play on the field. Salem's offense gained a first down, then stalled. After the Sailors kicked on fourth down, the ball came to rest on the Big Reds five-yard line.

Surprisingly, the visitors stopped the Brasher single wing cold. Once again, Brasher waved Chip in for Rankin. Standing in the end zone, Chip had a premonition of bad luck, of a blocked kick. But he got the ball away, hurrying the timing a little, lifting the ball off his toe just under the raised arms of Salem's left tackle.

Biggie Cohen made the tackle right in the center of the field, smack on the fifty-yard line. It was a beautiful kick, high and long, and the fans gave Chip a big hand. But that was the last applause Chip or the Big Reds got for a long time. Brasher made a mistake and sent in the second platoon, the Big Reds reserves. Salem promptly marched down the field against the second team, scoring in exactly five plays. Then the Sailors kicked the extra point to tie the score and buried Brasher's two-platoon system right then and there, forever.

Brasher rushed Rankin and the regulars back into the game, but it was too late. Salem had tasted blood and played inspired football, thirsting to be the first team to upset the state champs.

At the half, the score was 7-7. The head coach, gone berserk, immediately demonstrated why he was poorly qualified for his job. Brasher strode up and down in front of the grouped players, berating them. Much of his talk was unfit for any athlete of any age to hear.

Chip didn't look up at the angry man, but several players eyed him with nearly open contempt. Biggie Cohen was one of these, his hamlike hands gripping the bench until his big, broad knuckles turned white under tanned skin. The Big Reds weren't used to this kind of treatment.

A PASS AND A PRAYER

Chip's thoughts, peculiarly enough, were of Rockwell. He was thinking just how the Rock would have handled this situation. Chip knew the procedure by heart because the Rock never deviated a second from schedule. He allowed the players a minute to trot off the field and get set in the locker room under the stadium. There would follow two minutes of silence and complete relaxation. The Rock would take over then, speaking calmly, reviewing the first half for two minutes, using a similar period to outline his plans for the second half, then talking to the quarterback for a couple of minutes, and devoting another minute to team talk and a final minute to complete relaxation. That left the Big Reds one minute to return to the field and three minutes to warm up for the second half.

Brasher probably would have been even more upset if he could have heard the fans. They were loudly criticizing his two-platoon system.

"Two platoons!" a high-pitched voice shrilled. "If that reserve team is the second platoon, I'll take the band!"

"Hey, you know something? We haven't thrown a pass yet! No wonder Salem's got our running plays stopped; they don't have to worry about passes."

"Hilton can pass! He'd run those Sailors dizzy! What's Brasher holdin' him out for?"

"This guy must not believe in open football. Passin' is the most important thing in the game."

"You can say that again! The colleges and the pros gain more yards in the air than they do on the ground!"

"Rockwell's *T* was good enough for me. This kind of football is like a pitcher's duel in a baseball game. Nothin' happens!"

Brasher was still ranting when the timekeeper's warning whistle sounded, and he kept up the tirade all the way out to the bench, stopping just long enough to speak briefly to Chip. "It's our choice this half, Hilton," he growled, "and we'll kick. You go out there and tell the ref. This time, remember to stay out there for the kickoff."

The Big Reds joined Chip seconds later, muttering, grumbling, and deliberately kicking up clumps of Rockwell's beautiful stadium sod.

Chip tried to pump them up, but the Big Reds had lost their drive; they were just going through the motions. That had never happened with the Rock. Coach Rockwell's teams were renowned for their second-half fight.

Chip sailed the ball to the goal line, but the Big Reds didn't tear downfield with their usual drive, and the Salem runner nearly got away, making it to the forty before he was downed. On the referee's whistle, Chip headed for the bench, passing Rankin without a glance.

The Big Reds fans got a terrific shock on the first play. The Salem quarterback faked twice out of the *T* and then hurled a missile right down the center and over Rankin's head. The ball nosed down, just in time to slip surely into the hungry fingers of a tall, long-legged Sailor, who easily outdistanced Rankin for the score. Before a lot of them had even returned to their seats, the confident Valley Falls fans were stunned along with their vaunted state champions. Salem led 13-7. It was little comfort that the try for the extra point was wide of the uprights.

Salem's kickoff was a long one, right to Rankin on the ten, and the stocky ball carrier shot straight up the field. But he didn't even reach the wedge his teammates had dropped back to form and barely made the twenty before he was submerged by a wave of eager Sailors.

Chip's spirits hit a new low because he could see Rankin had now lost control of the team, and the Big Reds were totally down. As their attack stalled, Chip kept edging forward until he was kneeling on the side-line, practically on the field. He could scarcely restrain the urge to rush out on the field until Brasher sent him in to punt from the twenty-five.

He angled a long spiral, which carried from the fifteen to Salem's thirty-five before it shot out of bounds. Then he reluctantly took off his helmet and despondently headed back to the bench. That ended the quarter, but it didn't end Chip's anxiety. Time was against the Big Reds.

The stands were quiet, too quiet. There wasn't much to cheer about, and as Salem started a steady fourth-quarter drive, the shrill pleas of the cheerleaders to "hold that line" were ignored. When the Sailors reached the seven, first down and goal to go, their attack stalled.

The Big Reds held, taking over the ball on the one-yard line. Depressed as they were, the home supporters cheered that stand and began a chant of hope now that Valley Falls, at last, had the ball.

The goal-line stand seemed to carry over into the Big Reds' offense as well, and they tore into Salem with their old power. But the Sailors bottled them up, knowing Valley Falls had no passer. They concentrated their strength against Valley Falls's ground attack, stopping the Big Reds three straight times. Biggie Cohen took a deep, bitter breath and then called time.

Brasher's face was fiery red, and his constant verbal abuse could be heard in the stands. He stalked up and down in front of the bench, muttering and cursing, and finally stopped directly in front of Chip. "This is your doin', Hilton," he ranted. "You've been underminin' me ever since I took charge. For two cents I'd—"

Chip was shocked. Hard against his right arm, he felt Soapy poise for action. But the angry man controlled his fury and, after stalking away and then back again, sent Chip in to punt.

Chip's legs dragged. This was the first time he had ever dogged it going out on the field. But as he neared his teammates and saw the despair in their eyes, his leadership ignited, and he was once more the fighting captain of the state champs.

"Come on, guys," he barked. "This game isn't over!" In the huddle, he pounded his right fist into his left hand and spat out his words. "Quit fighting if you want to, but I'm not giving up! Come on! Give me a good line and a count of three before you go down! Another thing! I bet I make the tackle!"

Chip's challenge brought a chorus of protests and derisive sounds, and Chip knew his teammates were back in the groove, back in a fighting mood. The line broke out of the huddle, and the players dug in with their cleats while Chip backed up just short of the end line. He glanced at his backfield blockers. They were all set, poised to give him a good kicking lane.

Chip chanted out the signals and, as the ball came spinning back, rocked back on his left foot. He caught the ball, waist-high, and started the forward rocker just as Cody Collins met the charging left end with a vicious shoulder block that flattened the Sailor. A tall Sailors right end had knifed in, but Chris Badger knocked his feet out from under him as though he'd been cut down with a scythe. That left a gaping hole in the left side of the line. Chip and Speed saw it at the same time.

Speed, not hesitating a second, flashed through the hole and headed into the defensive secondary. It seemed to Chip then that everything worked just as if he had called the play. Just as they had worked Rockwell's fake punt play so many times, he faked the kick and followed

A PASS AND A PRAYER

Speed. Slicing behind a flying Morris, Chip grunted with satisfaction as Speed floored the nearest Sailor, leaving him in an open field. Chip galloped for the left sideline with powerful strides.

The last Salem defender had maneuvered Chip toward the sideline, but he hadn't counted on Chip's deceptive speed and realized too late he hadn't closed the gate. There was still a lane between himself and the sideline, and the runner was moving toward it like a runaway horse. The Sailors safety made the first move, streaking toward the tall speedster and diving across his path. All he hit was the green sod, sliding across the limed sideline in front of the Big Reds runner, who had hesitated before speeding across the broad-striped goal line to tie up the score, 13-13. Seconds later, Chip kicked the extra point, and the Big Reds led 14-13.

Chip trotted back toward the forty-yard line for the kickoff, trying to escape his teammates' happy mauling yet thrilling to the long "Yea, Hilton! Yea, Chip! Yea, Chip Hilton!" that came rolling across the stadium.

But it didn't last, didn't even last until he reached the center of the field. Tug Rankin came dashing in, waving Chip toward the sideline where Tom Brasher stood with his hands on his hips, his face twisted and disfigured by angry passion.

"That's enough, Hilton," he snarled, seizing Chip by the arm, his tongue bitter with anger. "You've gone too far this time! And for the last time! *I ordered you to kick!* You hear? I ordered you to kick! You deliberately disobeyed, deliberately challenged my orders. A real football player understands discipline, follows orders. You don't understand anything but press clippings and cheers. Leave the field, grandstander, and turn in your uniform. You're through! Understand? Dropped from the squad!"

CHAPTER 11

A Sailor Blooper

TUG RANKIN was just as surprised as Chip when Brasher sent him into the game. The new senior disliked Chip intensely, chiefly because Tom Brasher had filled his mind with false impressions about the Big Reds captain. Rankin had been determined to beat Chip out for the quarterback job, not only because he loved to play football and didn't like Chip, but because Brasher wanted it that way. Rankin felt indebted to Brasher and wanted desperately to please the burly coach. But Tug couldn't understand Brasher's sudden decision. Tug had been on his feet cheering just as madly as the rest of the bench when Chip sped down the field. He also knew Chip was the only decent kicker on the squad. But the broad-shouldered quarterback followed orders and trotted out to face the puzzled Big Reds.

"Coach said for you to kick, Cohen," Rankin said tersely.

"Me!" Biggie blurted. "Why me? What's wrong with Chip? I can't kick!"

"Chip must be hurt!" Soapy anxiously motioned toward the end of the field. "Look, Pop's taking him out of the stadium."

"He didn't act like he was hurt," Morris announced and swung abruptly around to face Rankin. "You know anything about this, Rankin?" he demanded.

Rankin glared at Morris and shook his head. "No. Why should I? Come on. Let's play!"

The Big Reds lined up, and Biggie plunked his foot into the ball with all his might, but his heavy leg lacked speed and follow-through, and the kick carried only to the Salem twenty. The Sailors fullback picked the ball out of the air on the dead run, but it slipped through his hands. Recovering the ball, he made it to the thirty before he was downed.

In the huddle, Rankin called for a seven-two-two defensive formation. That was a mistake. Salem's crafty, observant coach knew the Valley Falls personnel far better than the Big Reds new acting coach. Seconds before, he had watched Chip move slowly along the sideline and out the players gate leading to the practice field on the hill and to the locker rooms under the school gym. He didn't know why Hilton was leaving the field, but he knew the tall, lanky player was the only passer and kicker the Big Reds had. That was all he needed to know. A substitute dashed out on the field and into the Salem huddle.

Chip and Pop had emerged from the players gate and reached the upper field overlooking the concrete stadium just when the two teams broke out of their huddles. They paused to watch the action.

Chip sensed the play before the snap, and his warning shout made Pop jump. But it was useless; he was too far away. The crowd's noise would have drowned him out even if he'd been on the bench. Rankin was asleep on defense and came to life too late to do anything except turn and madly chase the receiver down the field. The alert Sailors quarterback had faked a run, drawing Tug up to the line, and then cleverly tossed the ball neatly over Tug's head to the wide open receiver. The whole Big Reds team was after the runner. Speed lunged at the tiring Sailor, causing him to stumble at the ten-yard line. The ball squirted loose and bounced uncertainly until Biggie fell on it at the three. Speed had saved a certain touchdown, but the Big Reds were backed against their own goal line.

Up on the hill, Chip and Pop looked at each other with shocked eyes, but neither spoke. Chip knew his teammates were really in a tough spot now. Their attack had been stalled all afternoon, and it would be expecting too much for the plays to start clicking all at once. He watched anxiously as the Big Reds came out of the huddle and into Brasher's single wing. They came out three straight times without gaining a yard. The fourth time, after a time-out, they lined up with Speed in punt formation.

Chip didn't want to watch the next play, but he was mesmerized. He knew how Speed must feel standing in the end zone, facing a nine-man Sailors rush. Yes, Salem could afford to gamble. The Sailors knew all about the Big Reds running back, knew he was a great runner and a deadly tackler, but also knew his limitations. They knew he couldn't pass and couldn't punt, so they concentrated on blocking the kick.

Rankin's voice came echoing out of the big concrete stadium, and on the snap Chip closed his eyes. He never saw the surge of the Salem line and the breakthrough that sent four blue-clad visitors driving straight up the kicking lane. But he heard the double thump—the thump of Speed's foot on the ball and the thump when it rebounded from a blue-clad chest. Chip's heart leaped, and his eyes shot open just in time to see the ball spinning wildly along the ground. A mob of blue- and red-clad figures pounced on the ball and became a mass of heaving, clawing players.

Chip's hopes rose as he watched the referee wade into the pile. He knew Speed and one or two other Big Reds were battling in that nearly all-blue mass of figures. But either way it was bad and would put Salem out in front. It had to be either a safety or a touchdown. Then the referee stepped out of the pile and shot his hands into the air. Salem was ahead 19-14.

Chip tried to turn away but couldn't. He stood rooted, bound by the tension of the drama down on the field. This extra point was vital. A successful try could practically put the game on ice for Salem, which meant his teammates would have to score twice since there was no one left to kick the point after a touchdown. Chip tried to estimate the time remaining to play. It couldn't be long. Salem had strangled Brasher's offensive attack, which made even one, much less two, scores by Valley Falls seem impossible.

The home fans had been stunned by the sudden reversal of fortunes. They'd sensed the importance of the play and had stood in dismayed silence when the blocked kick resulted in a Salem touchdown. They remained tense and frustrated as the suspense mounted when the two teams lined up for the try for point.

Biggie Cohen brought them out of their lethargy when he broke through the right side of Salem's line to block the kick. On the way, Biggie smashed right through the opposing linemen, and then, with his long arms extended high above his head, simply drove two of Salem's backs right into the kicker with his tree-trunk thighs. The ball rebounded from Biggie's chest all the way back to the twenty-yard line. Without losing a single stride, the bull-like rush of the big tackle propelled him through the kicker and after the flying ball. Cohen was all alone when he fell on the ball, but he wasn't taking any chances. He curled around the ball and covered it with his big hands until the referee's whistle ended the play.

The home fans cheered that break, giving Biggie a big hand when he signaled the referee that Valley Falls would receive. But the lift was only temporary, and fans' hearts were heavy as they studied the 19-14 score and the four minutes left on the clock. Chip was worried too. He watched the teams line up for the kickoff. He couldn't see the clock, but he knew time was running out.

The kick was a good one, with plenty of height, carrying to the five where Tug Rankin waited, poised for the catch. Chip was concentrating on the five Big Reds spread across the field just beyond the forty, and he thrilled at their speed in dropping back with the kick and their skill in forming the apex of the wedge. But just as before, their savvy went unused. Rankin lacked Chip's ability to speed past the first wave of converging tacklers. He never reached his interference, swamped hard on the nineteen under a swarm of blue shirts.

Standing high above the stadium and looking down over the edge of the concrete bowl, Chip saw a scout's view when he eyes an opponent. He felt like yelling for Rankin to call for a pass. Salem's seven-man line, with its diamond-shaped alignment of the backs was a perfect setup for almost any kind of pass. Salem's little quarterback was playing his safety position correctly, but his defensive backs were stationed no more than three yards behind the line of scrimmage.

Chip groaned. Any kind of a pass would click, but a running play would be smothered. Salem's defense consisted of a ten-man line with a little, skinny back playing safety and assuming the sole responsibility of covering the entire passing territory. Surely Rankin could throw some kind of pass!

But Rankin followed orders. Brasher didn't believe in throwing the ball. Tug sent Speed Morris driving into the line. With the possible threat of a pass, Salem's linemen might have been spaced a little more, the backs a little deeper. But Salem was gambling that Valley Falls would stick to its running attack, and the gamble worked. Speed was stopped at the line of scrimmage, cut down just as if he had hooked his neck into a clothesline. Rumbles of discontent intensified through the student sections. Chip, way up on the hill, could hear the chant almost as well as the players on the field.

"We want a touchdown! We want a touchdown! We want a touchdown!"

There was other chanting too. But it came from the less excitable and more discerning Big Reds fans.

"Pass that ball! Pass that ball! Pass that ball!"

It was all in vain. A reverse and a complicated lateral pass play designed to shake Morris loose failed to gain, and it was fourth and ten on the nineteen.

Chip could see Biggie and Speed talking to Rankin and gesturing toward the clock, and he knew exactly what it was all about. There wasn't much point in trying to hold the score down. The Rock always said, "One point or a hundred, what does it matter? Who won?"

Rankin must have won because the Big Reds slowly left the huddle and moved into punt formation. This time

A SAILOR BLOOPER

Speed got the kick away but not for much distance. The ball slithered off his toe and out of bounds on the thirty. There, with the jubilant roar from the visiting stands sweeping across the field, the Sailors took over.

Chip figured the visitors' cagey little quarterback would hold the ball, use all his available time, and run out the clock. But Chip was wrong. The Sailors had the state champs down and figured they might as well beat 'em good!

On the initial play, Salem made a first down, sweeping around J. P. Peck and going to the twelve before Speed Morris pulled the runner down from behind. The Sailors then discarded their huddle, desperate to score again on the state champs. Chip knew the Salem quarterback was running the plays in a series, desperate for a score.

The two lines merged and almost at the same instant, official time ran out. But the ball had already been snapped, and the play would be completed. The Sailors left halfback had the ball and was driving once more around Peck. Since it seemed all the Big Reds were on that side of the field, the runner reversed his direction and ran smack into Biggie Cohen.

Right then, the Sailors running back pulled one of those incomprehensible sports bloopers. He squirmed around in Cohen's arms and lateraled the ball toward a teammate. The outcome was so fast only a handful of spectators saw Speed Morris flash between the intended receiver and the runner and snatch the ball out of the air. The Big Reds supporters had turned disconsolately away and had headed for the exits. But they fought their way back when they heard a tremendous, deafening roar. They fought their way back to see Morris tearing up the field with the precious ball under his arm.

A PASS AND A PRAYER

There wasn't anyone in sight who could have caught Morris in his mad dash, even if he had started with the fleet speedster. That is, no one except Chip Hilton. Up on the practice field above the stadium, Chip was leaning forward yelling at the top of his voice.

"Go, Speed, go! Hurry! Hurry! Don't drop it, Speed," he pleaded, *"please!"*

Then Speed was over, and Chip caught Pop up in his arms, lifting his old friend high in the air. Suddenly, Chip thought of something and his eyes searched the field until he located each of the officials. He triumphantly yelled, "Touchdown!" and started on Pop again. The Big Reds had won, and Rock's "one or a hundred" suited Chip Hilton to a *T*. Heading for the dressing room, Pop and Chip didn't need to see the final score on the scoreboard: Visitors 19, Valley Falls 20.

"What happened to you?" Speed shouted. "You have trouble with Brasher?"

Chip shook his head. "No," he said slowly, "I didn't have any trouble."

Biggie Cohen enveloped Chip's chin in one of his massive paws and tilted his friend's face up to the light. "You sick?" he asked solicitously.

Chip grinned. "I was till Speed crossed that goal line!"

"What happened?" Speed persisted. "We needed you bad, and when we looked over to the bench, you were gone. I had to punt, and six hundred Sailors hit me and knocked me back fifteen yards.

"From now on I'm strictly a runner. I'm willing to do a little blocking, and I'll do my share of tackling. But kicking? No way! Not me! My kicking career finished this afternoon."

A SAILOR BLOOPER

The storm of good-natured joking the Big Reds gave Speed let Chip evade further questions. But he couldn't resist a grin at his own expense. Speed and his teammates didn't know it, but Chip Hilton's career had finished that afternoon too.

Cruising along in Morris's three-speed Mustang, Chip kept changing the subject, talking about Speed's great run and Biggie's smashing tackles. All the time, he was trying to figure out how he was going to keep his friends from learning the news. Pop Brown promised to say nothing, but Chip knew things like that were not easily kept secret. He'd have to do something before Monday. Maybe Coach Stewart would know what to do. He'd see Chet first thing after church on Sunday morning. Right now, he'd have to be clever, or one of his friends would pin him down and find out he'd been dropped from the squad. He could dodge them easily enough tonight at the Sugar Bowl by spending the evening cleaning up the basement, but he'd definitely have to see Chet tomorrow.

Later that evening, an argument was taking place that Chip would have found interesting. The lively Saturday night parties at Jerry Davis's house were important in promoting his status as the leader of Valley Falls's younger business community. Tonight, Tom Brasher and Muddy Waters had been special guests. After the other guests departed, the three met in Jerry's study to discuss their plan to take over the Big Reds athletics program.

Davis and Waters were deeply troubled because Brasher had dropped Hilton from the squad. Brasher's shortcomings were obvious, and they worried that his uncontrollable anger might completely ruin their plans.

A PASS AND A PRAYER

When Davis had first enlisted Waters's support, the reporter couldn't come up with a way to attack Rockwell. The veteran coach was surrounded by friends. Zimmerman, the principal, was Mayor Condon's tool, but he liked Rockwell and wasn't strong enough to challenge the coach. That left only Chet Stewart, Rockwell's first assistant. But Stewart was completely loyal. He'd played for Rockwell and worked with him for several years. His integrity was beyond reproach. Davis had been stymied until Brasher arrived on the scene.

Tom Brasher was their key. He was young, ambitious, and unscrupulous. Jerry Davis completely dominated him. Waters had built his attack around Brasher, his willing accomplice. He used his sports column to strengthen Brasher while persistently attacking Rockwell.

Now, just when everything seemed to be working according to plan, Brasher's vicious temper and unreasonable dislike for Chip Hilton were jeopardizing the whole scheme. The spiteful coach had let his hate for the Big Reds captain interfere with the chief objective. Getting rid of Coach Henry Rockwell was the important goal. The loss of Hilton could very well prevent that goal from being obtained.

At that afternoon's game, Waters and Davis had watched the crowd. Chip Hilton was respected on and off the field. They hadn't missed the sideline incident when Brasher ordered Chip to the locker room. They'd listened to their accomplice's version of the story on the way home. They knew Brasher had made a mistake. Brasher's continued abuse of the all-state star would be disastrous.

Waters and Davis also realized Chip Hilton's timely run had saved the day. They knew, too, that Brasher was too bullheaded to accept the fact. Neither was sold on Tug Rankin, and both doubted that Brasher could win games without Chip Hilton in uniform. After hearing the fans' comments, they were convinced Brasher had gone too far. Somehow, the difficulties between Brasher and the veteran quarterback had to be patched up. They'd engineered Brasher into this meeting and were maneuvering him to change his mind.

"Look, Tom," Davis said patiently, "I've got more reason to dislike the kid than you have. I'm not sticking up for him. He's secondary. Rockwell's our target! You can't seem to get that through your head. Hilton's a senior. It's his last year. But Rockwell might hold on for years unless we put you in so tight right now that the fans won't want him back. Understand?"

Brasher scowled and shook his head. "No, I don't. One minute you say you don't want the kid and want me to handle it and the next minute you say to lay off. What do you want? The smart aleck tried to make me look stupid. He refused to follow orders when I told him to kick, didn't he? You don't think I'm gonna take that, do you? Nothin' doin'!"

"We know how you feel, Tom," Waters said softly, "but Hilton's admired here, and you'll have them all down on you if you're not careful. Despite your instructions to kick, the fact remains he won the game. And that's important!"

"I'll say it is," Davis added. "You've got to win here. I know. I've lived here all my life. You keep winning, and they'll go along with you, but once you start losing, they'll start hollering for Rockwell. Stay calm. Keep Hilton on the squad. Give him a tough way to go but keep him around until you're established. Then dump him."

"If you think I'm gonna ask that jerk back, you're crazy," Brasher snarled. "Not for this job or ten jobs! He'll have to crawl to me."

CHAPTER 12

Personal Accountability and Faith

MARY HILTON knew something was up. Early that morning, she'd read the sports pages. She knew as soon as Chip came into the kitchen his cheerfulness was a mask of his true feelings. She greeted him tenderly, checked on the chocolate cake in the oven, fed Hoops, and turned the conversation to the home repairs needed before winter. Each knew the other was fencing, avoiding references to the subject disturbing them most, and finally Chip brought it up.

"I guess you read the papers," Chip said tentatively, anxiously watching his mother's face.

"Yes," Mary Hilton said brightly, "I read them, read both of them. Mr. Williams said you won the game."

"Guess you read what Muddy Waters had to say."

"Yes, I did, Chip. I always read his articles, but I don't put much faith in what he writes."

Chip glumly pushed lunch around his plate, his troubled gray eyes reflecting the discouragement written so deeply in his heart. Every word of Waters's column burned deeply in his memory, burned there so deeply he didn't think he'd ever forget them. He couldn't understand why his mom was so unconcerned.

"Guess you read I'd been dropped from the squad for insubordination."

"Yes, I read it, but I don't believe it."

"But it's true, Mom. It's true!"

"For insubordination, Chip? I think I know you better than that."

"Well, it wasn't insubordination, Mom."

"Then there's nothing to worry about, Chip. If you were wrong and Coach Brasher was right, you owe an apology to the coach."

"But, Mom, I never dreamed the coach meant for me to kick, no matter what happened. Football wouldn't be football if everyone knew exactly what the other team or player was going to do."

"Maybe not, Chip, but when the coach instructs a player to do something, isn't it only fair for a player to follow those instructions? Or at least try to follow them?"

"Yes, Mom, and I did try to kick. Only there was such a big hole there, and, well, it was the right thing to do!"

Mary Hilton's gray eyes warmed suddenly, and she came over behind Chip and placed her hands on his shoulders. "Never mind, Chipper," she said understandingly. "Let's let the situation figure itself out. I'm sure you never meant to deliberately go against the coach, and I'm sure you'll do the right thing."

Chip rose to his feet and kissed his mom lightly on the cheek. He headed to his room, stopping on the way to pick up the sports pages of the *Times* and the *Post*. He wanted to read Waters's story again. Later, stretched out on his bed listening to music, he reviewed the game once again, trying to put all the pieces of his shattered football problem into place.

Tom Brasher was on his case just as Soapy and Speed and Biggie and Red kept saying. But what could he do about it? He hadn't meant to cross Brasher up on that play, and he hadn't tried to make the new coach angry at him that day at Midwestern. The Rock had always instructed his players to take advantage of every break that came along, and when that hole had opened up, he'd acted almost without thinking. He'd even started his rocker motion for the kick.

But it wasn't any time to be thinking about himself. The only thing that mattered right now was Coach Rockwell. He'd do anything he could to keep the Rock from getting upset and worsening his condition. Even if he had to apologize to Brasher.

After dinner that evening, Chip sat in front of his computer, finishing his U.S. history work. He was the only member of the Hilton A. C. who wasn't at the Sugar Bowl that evening.

Petey Jackson was curious about the meeting being held behind closed doors in the storeroom. He leaned dejectedly on the counter and wondered what was going on. If Petey could have seen Soapy Smith pacing back and forth, reading Muddy Waters's story, he'd have known what was up.

"Listen to this!" Soapy exploded, shaking the paper viciously. "Listen! 'Modern football has come to Valley Falls with the appointment of Tom Brasher as coach of the Big Reds football team—'"

"Modern football!" Schwartz snorted sarcastically. "Hah!"

Soapy continued, "'The platoon system has been needed at Valley Falls for many years, and Coach Brasher's desire to adopt this phase of up-to-date football is noteworthy and requires only a large player turnout to assure its success—'"

"Yeah, right!" Biggie muttered.

"'Chip Hilton, unable to handle the single-wing quarterback job, was used chiefly in the kicking department. Tug Rankin, the new quarterback find, was stellar. He handled the position with authority and demonstrated he is clearly the best blocker on the squad—'"

"There hasn't been a game played where he could block with Chip or Cody or Chris or—oh, what's the use," Speed declared heatedly.

"Hey! Get this," Soapy continued, glaring angrily at the paper. "'Every young coach finds it necessary to cope with undisciplined boys at some stage of his career. Coach Tom Brasher found it necessary to send Chip Hilton to the showers yesterday for insubordination. However, the Valley Falls captain will undoubtedly see the error of his ways and offer the new mentor an appropriate apology.'"

"Apology!" Morris grated. "What for?"

"Who could apologize to that guy!" Soapy demanded.

"Not me," Biggie Cohen said slowly. "I guess I'd better drop football. I figure Brasher can get along without someone like me if he can bench the best player in the state!"

Speed agreed. "Me too," he said hotly. "Come on. Let's go tell Chip!"

While all this was happening at the Sugar Bowl, Chip had been staring at the screen trying to come up with the conclusion to his paper. But football kept sweeping through his mind so often that he shut down the computer, laid aside his books, and sought comfort in reading Pete Williams's story in the *Post*.

BIG REDS DEFEAT SAILORS
GET BREAKS IN LAST-SECOND VICTORY

Valley Falls High School opened the football season yesterday afternoon by defeating Salem High School, 20-19, in a last-second thriller. The Big Reds were lucky to defeat a fighting bunch of Sailors who were after the first major upset of the new season. Two sensational runs saved the day, one by Captain Chip Hilton from deep in his own end zone and a last-second dash by Speed Morris following a nifty stolen lateral. Valley Falls owes the Salem quarterback a big thanks for his generous last-play lateral, which flew straight into the arms of the fastest man on the field— Speed Morris. (See the details of the game elsewhere on this page.)

The new single-wing formation resulted in another disorganized attack. It's hard to believe any attack limiting itself to a straight ground game can successfully cope with the defensive strength of present-day high school football.

And that brings up the subject of Chip Hilton. How can anyone overlook Hilton's passing, running, kicking, and general leadership? There isn't another high school player in the country so liberally endowed with those talents and abilities. It's hard to understand the disciplinary action of benching a player because he saw an opportunity to run for a touchdown instead of punting from behind his own goal line.

PERSONAL ACCOUNTABILITY AND FAITH

There was more to the column, but Chip tossed the paper aside. He was completely confused. Waters devoted his whole column to criticism of his play while Pete Williams took the opposite view. How could two sportswriters see the same game and write such divergent reviews?

Sitting at his desk, Chip was trying to figure a way out of his predicament when his mother called him. Chet Stewart was in the family room and wanted to speak to him.

Stewart's greeting was warm and friendly, but his eyes warned Chip of trouble. "I just saw Mrs. Rockwell, Chip," he said gravely, "and she tells me Rock isn't doing so well. That's why I'm here. We've got to keep the team together and keep the coach from hearing about all this football trouble. Thank goodness they have him isolated.

"I know how you feel about everything, Chip, but I want you to do all you can to keep the team fighting. I'm sure Brasher will get in touch with you in the next couple of days and straighten out your difficulties."

"I'll do my part, Coach," Chip said earnestly. "I really didn't intend to disobey instructions, but the hole opened up so fast that before I knew it, I was running."

"I understand, Chip," Stewart assured him, "but I just wanted to be sure the rest of the team didn't get in an uproar, especially right now."

Stewart's timing couldn't have been better. His words were almost drowned out by the sound of tramping feet on the front porch and a mad rush through the hall. Soapy Smith led the charge into the family room.

"Hi, Coach. We didn't expect you to be here. What's up?"

"Something you ought to know about," Stewart said firmly. "All of you. Now quiet down and listen.

A PASS AND A PRAYER

"The Rock's pretty bad, and you guys have to pull together as a team and be sure there's no trouble with Brasher. I know what's been going on, but I'm taking it, and you're going to have to take it too. Chip's really been pushed around, but we can't do anything about that right now. We'll let that work itself out. How do you guys feel about it?"

Stewart found that out! Their responses were blunt and defiant. Then for almost two hours he and Chip argued, reasoned, and pleaded with the rebellious group. In the end the duo won, but it wasn't a complete victory. Cohen summed up the squad's feelings as they were leaving. They'd stick it out with Brasher for another week, but if Chip wasn't reinstated by then, they were turning in their uniforms.

Monday passed slowly for Chip. He waited all day for a message calling him to Brasher's office but heard nothing. After his last class, he talked briefly with Soapy, then walked slowly down to the practice field and sat down on the first row of bleachers. He'd just dropped his books onto the seat when Brasher appeared and strode straight toward him.

"Look, Hilton," Brasher snarled, "you're not wanted here as a spectator or as a player until you're ready to apologize. That what you came for, to apologize?"

"I—I wanted to watch practice."

"That's what you think! You're not watching my practices! Get out and stay out until you're ready to apologize. Do you understand?"

Chip tried to force words of apology through his lips, but they just wouldn't come.

"Well, get goin'!" Brasher bellowed. "And keep goin'!"

Chip's cheeks burned, but he walked carefully around Brasher and headed for the hill. Bitter, angry words rushed to escape his lips, but he held them in and silently trudged up the incline and out the steel gate beside the gym. There he leaned against the wall. If he'd been given the chance, he would have apologized to Brasher down there on the practice field. He'd have taken Brasher's belittling and would even have apologized in front of his teammates. But despair and growing resentment toward Brasher fought Chip's thoughts of reconciliation.

That night after work, he confided the details of the afternoon's events to his mom. When he went to bed, most of the hurt in his heart had been eased by his mother's understanding sympathy.

Long after Chip had gone to bed, Mary Hilton sat downstairs searching for some way to help her son. Usually she let Chip stand on his own feet, solve his own problems, fight his own battles. But this was different. She didn't know exactly how her son had been drawn into the animosity between Jerry Davis and Henry Rockwell, but she sensed Chip's loyalty to his coach had something to do with it. Mrs. Hilton finally decided to see the school principal to find out why her son was being involved and why Tom Brasher so strongly opposed Chip.

Principal Zimmerman sat thinking about Chip and Mary Hilton for a full half-hour before their three o'clock appointment. Everyone in Valley Falls knew the story of Big Chip Hilton. One of the greatest athletes ever to play for the high school and the state university, Big Chip had become an athletic tradition. He had starred in three sports at State and had then returned to Mary Carson and Valley Falls with a degree in ceramics and a burning desire to be a great chemist. It hadn't been easy for the great athlete to turn down a professional sports career, but Big Chip Hilton had wanted a home with Mary Carson and a chance for a career in ceramics. He'd won on all counts. Mary Carson became Mary Hilton, and J. P. Ohlsen started Big Chip off as a chemist.

Twelve years later, Big Chip Hilton was Ohlsen's chief chemist, was teaching young Chip Hilton all about sports, and was dreaming of the day his old coach, Henry Rockwell, would have his son as a candidate for his teams. But he didn't live long enough to see that dream realized. Big Chip lost his life in a desperate attempt to save a careless workman from being crushed in one of the pottery kilns.

It had been a dreadful blow for Mary Hilton. But she was a champion too. She'd nurtured Chip's love of sports and provided him a role model of personal accountability and faith. Long before his time, Little Chip took on adult responsibilities.

Zimmerman admired Chip and he admired Mary Hilton. But his hands were tied too. He wouldn't be able to help her very much with this problem. That was what he told her a little later, carefully avoiding any references to the political pressure responsible for his helplessness, and gently suggested it would be better for everyone if Chip apologized to Tom Brasher.

Mary Hilton sensed Zimmerman was holding something back. She felt he was trying to convey a message he couldn't or wouldn't put into words.

"I'll talk to Chip, Mr. Zimmerman," she responded, "and thank you for your interest in—"

Zimmerman interrupted her. "Just a moment before you go, Mrs. Hilton. The students here at Valley Falls are my business. I've seen hundreds of them come and go, and I want you to know Chip is one of the finest young men I've ever had under my supervision. He's just a bit more impetuous than he should be perhaps, but he'll grow out of that, all right."

Zimmerman picked up a large card. "This is Chip's record, Mrs. Hilton. It contains all his grades for the past three years.

"Chip has maintained nearly a B+ average during those three years, in addition to participating in football, basketball, and baseball and working after school. Frankly, I don't know how he does it! Certainly much of the credit is yours, and I want to congratulate you on a splendid job."

"Thank you, Mr. Zimmerman. I am proud of Chip. He never complains about having to work, and he spends every minute possible with his books. About the only fun he has is in sports, and lately it hasn't been much fun for him. That's why I felt so strongly about seeing you. I don't know where he gets all his drive."

Zimmerman chuckled. "I know," he said softly, looking deeply into Mary Hilton's gray eyes. "I know exactly where he gets every good quality he possesses. And because of those qualities, I know every dream you have and every ambition he has will come true."

CHAPTER 13

True Champions Never Quit

MARY HILTON was like a second mom to Chip's friends. They respected and admired her. That was the reason Biggie Cohen, Speed Morris, and Red Schwartz responded eagerly to her phone call and gathered in the Hilton family room promptly at eight o'clock that night. When Chip's mom stated she felt Chip should apologize to Coach Brasher, she was surprised by their reaction.

"Mrs. Hilton," Biggie lamented, "it just isn't right."

"It sure isn't," Schwartz added dourly. "If there's any apologizing, Brasher ought to do it. Chip didn't do anything wrong, unless running for a touchdown is wrong."

"If we had our way, Brasher would have to apologize to the whole school," Speed asserted.

"Yes, and if the Rock wasn't so sick, Rankin would be talking to himself every night out on the practice field," Biggie said dryly. "We'd have walked out on him a week ago if Chip hadn't made us promise to wait until Coach Rockwell got out of the hospital."

Mary let them talk before telling them Chip was wrong in principle, that discipline is vital even in the face of defeat. Even when they agreed Chip should apologize, she sensed they were cooperating because they believed apologizing was the expedient thing for him to do and not because it was the right thing. After they'd left, she wondered, too, whether she was doing the right thing in trying to get Chip to say he was sorry for something when he didn't really feel that way.

Biggie, Speed, and Red drove dejectedly away from the Hilton home with the same feeling.

"We'll have to be subtle about this," Biggie warned.

"Right!" Speed agreed. "We'd better keep this between us."

"Personally," Schwartz said decisively, "I'd rather we all walked out right now. If it wasn't for Chip and the Rock, I'd drop football tonight. I'll be glad when Coach gets back on his feet!"

After Chip, Biggie Cohen was the natural leader of the Hilton A. C., and he took charge and made the plans. Chip was surprised at the change in his friends' attitudes. Biggie was the first to arrive at the Sugar Bowl and, after reviewing the day's workout, let Chip know things weren't going so well.

"The guys are pretty upset," he confided, "and almost anything could happen the way practices are going. I sure wish there was some way you could get back on the squad."

Just before closing time, Speed Morris and Red Schwartz joined Chip, Soapy, and Petey Jackson at the counter. There wasn't a customer in the place, and Petey immediately directed the conversation toward the big problem. "How you guys gettin' along with Brasher?"

"What do you think?" Schwartz demanded. "Without Chip out there, it isn't the same. I don't think we can take it much longer. In fact, if Brasher doesn't do something about Chip in a hurry, he isn't going to have a football team unless Rankin plays every position at the same time."

"You can say that again!" Speed added.

Chip studied his friends intently. "Look," he said anxiously, "you guys said you were going to stick it out until the Rock got better."

"That's good, coming from you," Speed retorted. "That's easy enough to say when you don't have to be out there every day and take the grief Brasher hands out. I've taken just about all I can take."

Chip was completely alarmed now. Things must be bad. He'd better get back on the squad before it was too late! If there was only some way without apologizing to Brasher. He just couldn't bring himself to do it! There would just have to be some other way. But after a sleepless night, he decided there was no other way except to apologize to Brasher.

Wednesday morning, he appeared in Zimmerman's office and told him he would like to apologize to Brasher. Zimmerman knew how Chip felt and spared him considerable embarrassment by calling Tom Brasher and telling him that Chip Hilton was in his office. He was sending Chip down to the athletics office and hoped the difficulty could be worked out.

Chip had never dreaded anything more in his life than this meeting with Brasher. He knocked on the door to the athletics office. He was nervous, but he was going to force himself to go through with this meeting. He stuck with his resolve and after the first few words was able to take Brasher's sneering acceptance of his apology without losing his self-respect. His head was high and his eyes steady when Brasher growled that he could put on a uniform.

Chip kept the good news to himself through his morning classes, lunch, and the afternoon classes, but somehow the guys had heard about it and were waiting when he walked into the locker room.

"All right, Chip!" Soapy yelled. "How about a cheer!"

But Chip stopped that. "Skip it," he said brusquely. "You act as though I'd just run for a touchdown!"

It wasn't long before Chip was running for touchdowns, because that evening, in the intrasquad scrimmage, he was once again the elusive, broken-field runner who had created such a sensation throughout the state the previous year. Brasher kept him with the reserves all that week, but Chip's play was inspirational and gave the squad the lift it needed.

On Saturday morning, the Big Reds piled onto the bus for their trip to Hampton. Chet Stewart was the last to climb aboard, and as the bus pulled away, Chip saw Tom Brasher and Muddy Waters get into Jerry Davis's car. As the Cadillac roared away, Chip grinned wryly. The Rock always rode with the team.

Out on the field, Chip was booming his warm-up punts. A little later, with Speed holding the ball, he was hitting his place kicks regularly from the thirty-five.

Standing out in the middle of the field with the Hampton captain felt great. When he called tails on the coin flip and won, Chip said the Big Reds would kick off. Chip pumped his foot into the ball a few seconds later, sending it end over end, straight as an arrow, over the goal line and beyond the end zone. Then he turned and saw Tug Rankin hustling onto the field.

A PASS AND A PRAYER

Somehow, Chip didn't feel so unhappy about the substitution this time. He pulled off his helmet and trotted over to the bench, dropping down beside Soapy. There the two friends, shoulder to shoulder, found understanding and strength in their friendship, and with that spirit warming their hearts, they sat quietly watching the game.

Hampton put the ball in play on the twenty-yard line and launched a determined attack against the middle of the Valley Falls line. When the Big Reds closed in, the Hampton quarterback opened them up with a pass, and before the game was three minutes old, the Big Reds were backed up against their own goal line, and Hampton was knocking at the door. Rankin called time, but it didn't stop the momentum of the attack. Hampton scored seconds after play was resumed on a pass into the end zone. The tall, rangy Hampton end seemed to use Tug Rankin as a ladder when he climbed high in the air and brought down the ball for the touchdown.

Seconds later, the attempted kick for the extra point was blocked when the ball clumped against Biggie Cohen's chest. Hampton led 6-0.

The Hampton kick was high and long, down to the five, but Speed made it back to the fifteen. But that was as far as the Big Reds could get. After three running plays were smothered, Brasher sent Chip racing in to punt.

Chip got a good one away down to the Hampton forty, and Biggie Cohen dropped the ball carrier there. Then Chip trotted off the field, and Hampton promptly marched down to the twenty before giving up the ball on downs.

For three long periods that was the story of the game. The Big Reds couldn't gain an inch, and Hampton couldn't get past the twenty. The Valley Falls line was fighting for all it was worth, and the driving attack of the Hampton line had slowed down to a walk.

TRUE CHAMPIONS NEVER QUIT

The game became a punting duel with Chip gradually forcing Hampton deep into its own territory. Time after time, he angled the ball out of bounds inside the ten-yard line. Then, early in the fourth quarter, Chip bounced one out of bounds on the Hampton three-yard line. It was a beautiful fifty-yard kick and brought a roar of applause from both stands. But the Hampton quarterback made the fans forget Chip's punt a few seconds later by hurling a long pass far over Rankin's head and into the eager fingers of his long-legged left end. The big end practically waltzed the length of the field and Hampton led 12-0. Biggie Cohen again blocked the attempt for the extra point.

Chip and Soapy were on their feet yelling encouragement to their teammates when Brasher grasped each by an arm. "Get in there, you two," he bellowed. "Smith, left end! Hilton, for Rankin!" He gave them a violent shove, adding, "See if you can get our running attack going."

The complexion of the game changed immediately. Hampton kicked the ball right down the middle to the ten, and Chip took it on the dead run, picking up the wedge on the twenty-five and going all the way to the forty. It was the first Big Reds yardage of the game.

Chip, in the huddle, called for Rockwell's reverse-pass play, the play he had made history with as a sophomore. The ball came shooting back, and Chip started to his right, suddenly reversed himself, swung to the left, picked up Badger and Morris for interference, and ran to the left sideline. There he stabbed his front foot hard into the soft turf and hurled the ball far down the field, far over the head of the Hampton safety and into the arms of Red Schwartz. Red hugged the ball and crossed the goal line untouched. A moment later, with Speed holding, Chip nailed the extra point, and the score was Hampton 12, Valley Falls 7.

A PASS AND A PRAYER

Hampton called a time-out, and the Big Reds trotted to the sideline in front of the bench and formed a circle.

Chip glanced at Brasher. The surly coach was watching the Hampton huddle across the field and talking fast.

"Stay in there, Hilton. And kick that ball right over the stadium," he muttered.

This was more like it. Maybe Brasher was really going to give him a chance.

He got a little too far under the ball, and it carried only to the five, but as it turned out, it worked better for him, as Nick Trullo smeared the Hampton receiver on the twelve. After the tackle, Chip was pumped, but his elation died when he saw Tug Rankin loping toward him. Chip again returned to the bench and dropped down, sick at heart. But he was right up again, for Hampton fumbled and Soapy recovered.

"All right, Soapy!" he yelled. "Way to go!"

This was the break of the game, and every Valley Falls player and fan knew it. "We want a touchdown! We want a touchdown!" chanted the Big Reds fans. "Hold that line! Hold that line!" pleaded the Hampton stands. Hampton held. Three straight times without giving up an inch.

Chip was desperate. "I can kick a field goal, Coach," he blurted, "I know I can!"

Brasher withered him with a contemptuous look. "What good's three points?"

"But there's still time, Coach," Chip pleaded, gesturing toward the clock. "There's still four minutes to go."

Brasher surprised himself then. He wondered later what had caused him to make the decision. "All right," he grated, "go in and kick!"

Chip drove the ball straight between the uprights to make the score Hampton 12, Valley Falls 10.

Again Chip smacked the ball into the end zone and trotted to the sideline passing Rankin on the way without a word. Hampton took no chances this time and kept the ball on the ground. The Valley Falls line held, and Hampton punted on fourth down. Chip looked at the clock—three minutes left to play.

The Big Reds couldn't gain a first down, and once more Brasher sent Chip in to kick. "Go in and kick that ball out of bounds," he growled. "We've gotta play for the breaks!"

Chip kicked the ball out of bounds on the twenty-one and again passed Rankin on his way toward the bench.

"On again, off again," Soapy muttered. "What is this, a relay team? You and Rankin ought to have a baton!"

Chip never heard Soapy, nor did anyone else on the Big Reds bench. The Hampton quarterback fumbled the snap, and Lou Mazotta fell on the ball on the twenty-two-yard line. One continuous roar erupted from the Valley Falls stands, but the cheers changed to groans when Rankin used three straight plunges into the line for no gain. Then, when Tug called for a time-out, the Big Reds fans began a familiar chant. "We want Hilton! We want Hilton! We want Hilton!"

"Please, Coach," Chip pleaded, "let me try another field goal!"

Brasher studied the scoreboard. There was less than a minute to play. "All right," he snapped. "But don't miss!"

Chip didn't miss. The ball split the uprights and Valley Falls led 13-12. There was time left for the kickoff, but the Big Reds swarmed all over Hampton on the last two plays, not giving the opponents an inch. Time expired, and Biggie Cohen grabbed the ball and started a snake dance.

A PASS AND A PRAYER

Brasher put a stop to the celebrating. He charged out on the field, ordering the team to the locker room, and bellowed angrily. "Break it up! That was the worst exhibition I ever saw! Get to the locker room! We're starting home right now! This doesn't call for a celebration! That was the worst football I ever saw!"

CHAPTER 14

Down but
Not Out

MONDAY AFTERNOON, Brasher ordered a scrimmage and placed Chip and Soapy with the reserves. Chip kicked off, and right on the first play, on the kickoff, Chip cut Rankin down on the fifteen-yard line with a powerful tackle that caused the husky quarterback to fumble the ball. Rankin stayed down, stretched out on the field. Then Brasher came streaking across the field and headed straight for Chip.

"What are you tryin' to do, Hilton?" he demanded harshly. "This is a practice scrimmage! Besides, you hit him after the play was over."

There was dead silence. Every player on the field knew the coach's accusation was false. Chip didn't say a word, but he was doing plenty of thinking. What was he supposed to do, play tag? Well, if that's what Brasher wanted.

A few minutes later, Rankin cut around left end behind perfect interference and got into the open field. Chip cut across the field and caught up with Tug but made no attempt to tackle him, just slapped him on the shoulder. But Rankin didn't stop. He continued running downfield until he was jarred to a vicious stop by Soapy's tackle. Soapy wasn't going to play tag.

Then the regulars started playing tag, simply going through the motions, tapping runners instead of tackling them. But Rankin didn't play tag. He kept driving everything toward Chip, trying his best to clip Chip on every play. But he didn't reach the Big Reds captain. Chip merely sidestepped or leaped in the air, and the disgruntled quarterback landed flat on the ground time and again without once taking Chip out of a play or off his feet. Each time Rankin missed Chip, laughter erupted from the rest of the squad. Brasher and Rankin were both angry now, but neither seemed able to cope with the situation.

Minutes later, Chip punted, sprinted down the field, and tagged Rankin. Then Brasher lost his head, accused Chip of dogging it, showing off, and making a farce of the scrimmage.

"Well, say something, Hilton!" Brasher yelled. "Don't stand there! Say something!"

"I just thought you didn't want me to tackle hard," Chip managed. "You barked at me before because I hit him hard. I don't know what you want me to do."

"I want you to play football! Good, hard football!" Brasher yelled. "That's what I want you to do and you'd better do it!" He whipped around to the regulars. "And that goes for you too," he yelled savagely.

Chip was really bugged now, but he kept quiet, resolved to play as hard as he knew how. "This time I'll really hit him," he muttered, as he dropped back to punt.

He got off a long, high one and then dashed down the field, determined to make the tackle himself. Rankin caught the ball and started back along the right sideline.

DOWN BUT NOT OUT

But Soapy was coming right at him, and Tug cut toward the center of the field. He didn't get far. Chip hit him at full speed, knocking him clear out of bounds. Chip then winked at Soapy and started back to his defensive position. That was the reason he didn't see Rankin coming. Tug hit Chip right in the middle of the back and knocked the unsuspecting captain flat on his face.

Then Tug began to beat Chip unmercifully. Chip was taller but was greatly outweighed, and he had been caught by surprise. But in the brief second it took him to hurl himself sideways and twist free, Chip realized that Tug Rankin was stronger than he was. He got to his feet just in time to dodge another rush. Then his teammates grabbed Rankin, and Brasher was between the two players.

"I'll bring some boxing gloves out here tomorrow night," Brasher raged, "and the first time something like this happens again, you'll have to fight it out right here before the whole squad."

"Suits me," Rankin growled.

Chip said nothing. He wasn't worried about boxing Tug Rankin. Big Chip had taught him to box, and Chip had later worked out with the boxing instructor at the Y. He was fast, clever with his fists, and a good puncher. But angry as he was, Chip remembered his father's words of advice: "Fighting is necessary only as a last resort and as a means of protection. You should know how to defend yourself, and that's the reason I want you to learn."

Chip wasn't worried about Rankin's attacking him or worried about his ability to handle his heavier opponent, but he felt more secure and confident because he had had some experience with the gloves.

The incident ended the practice. Brasher angrily dismissed the squad with the usual. "All right, three laps and hit the showers!"

A PASS AND A PRAYER

That evening, Soapy managed to get away from the fountain counter and stand at the storeroom door when Chip turned on the radio for Stan Gomez's broadcast over WTKO. Petey was there, too, leaving the booths and tables unattended. It was a good thing John Schroeder didn't drop in at that moment, but maybe it wouldn't have mattered so much. The boss was also an avid sports fan.

"Welcome sports fans, this is Stan Gomez from WTKO, bringing you the seven o'clock sports news of Valley Falls, the state, and the nation.

"How about the great Steelers team, the Steeltown Iron Men! The Steelers have won three straight games by overwhelming margins and stack up undoubtedly as the strongest team in the state. Let's make a little comparison here. The Big Reds beat Salem in the first game of the season, 20-19. A week later, Steeltown beat the Sailors, 76-3. That gives you a pretty good idea of their power.

"This Saturday, October 8, the Big Reds play Stratford at home. On September 17, Steeltown defeated the Strats, 52-0. Valley Falls fans will have a chance to make another comparison this Saturday. Don't miss the game.

"The Big Reds are coming along slowly. They've been upset by their coach's illness, but there's good news on that tonight. Henry Rockwell has come through the crisis, and if everything turns out as Doc Jones believes, the old Rock will be back on the team within the next four weeks.

"Let's take a moment here to give a couple of plaudits to Tom Brasher and Chet Stewart who have carried on in the absence of the master. Come Saturday, November 19, I believe that Steeltown and Valley Falls will clash for the Section Two championship. Additionally, that game may also have a direct bearing on the state championship."

Soapy snapped off the radio. "We better win a few other games first," he muttered. "How about Southern,

Weston, Delford, and Hampton? He's countin' a lot of eggs before they're hatched!"

"You mean chickens before they're hatched, don't ya?" Petey joked. "Someday I'm gonna make a list of the best Soapyisms."

Chip and Soapy remembered Gomez's words the next Saturday afternoon. Stratford was tough! Steeltown might have walked all over the Strats and held them scoreless, but that was more than the Big Reds could do. The Strats jumped right out in front in the first quarter and led the Big Reds 14-0.

Chip hadn't even been in the game because the Big Reds had won the toss and had elected to receive. Then, after Valley Falls gave up two quick touchdowns, Chip realized something would have to be done fast, if his team was going to win.

Brasher's single-wing attack was going nowhere. The reason was obvious. Stratford knew Tug Rankin couldn't pass, and its defense was set up solely with the idea of stopping the Big Reds running game. Stop it Stratford did! At the half, when Brasher angrily led the team under the concrete stadium, the score was still Stratford 14, Valley Falls 0. Their dejected walk to the locker room marked the first time the Big Reds had crossed the fifty-yard line all afternoon!

Chip had heard stories about halftime orations, but he'd never experienced anything like the fifteen-minute barrage that followed. Brasher raged back and forth for the entire fifteen minutes. Not once did he offer anything constructive. Chip glanced at Coach Stewart. Chet, who had grown up under Henry Rockwell's coaching, must have been as shocked as Chip. Sitting with folded arms and looking down at the floor, Chet didn't even seem to be listening.

A PASS AND A PRAYER

Brasher's diatribe wasn't inspiring, but it roused the athletes, sending them out on the field full of rage. Brasher sent Chip in to kick and then immediately pulled him out. When the Big Reds got the ball, they started a determined march up the field, and the single wing, for the first time, began to roll up yardage. Stratford called time-out twice during the long march, but nothing could stop the Big Reds, and they scored their first touchdown in exactly eleven plays. Brasher sent Chip in to kick the extra point, making the score Stratford 14, Valley Falls 7.

Suddenly things began to happen. Stratford brought Chip's kickoff back to midfield and fumbled. Biggie pounced on the loose ball. On the first offensive play, Speed electrified the crowd by breaking away and going all the way to the Stratford thirty.

Football is like that. The team that has been clicking during most of the game suddenly loses the breaks and begins to falter. That's what happened to Stratford. Twice, Rankin fooled the Strats line, faking a handoff on each call to the crossing running backs. Valley Falls hammered the strong side of the line for two first downs and a touchdown seconds later when Speed skirted the left end. Then Chip booted the extra point. Stratford 14, Valley Falls 14.

The seesaw battle began again. Chip's long, booming punts began to tell. Stratford was driven back to its own goal. Finally, with two minutes left to play, the Big Reds stalled on the Stratford twenty, third down and ten. Brasher rushed along the bench and grabbed Chip roughly by the shoulder.

"Get in there, Hilton," he barked. "Go in for Rankin and move that ball into position for a field goal. It's our only chance."

DOWN BUT NOT OUT

Chip dashed onto the field and into the huddle and called his own signal. Cutting to the right, he was downed in front of the goal on the seventeen. Then, with Speed holding, Chip dropped back his usual nine yards and coolly knocked the three-pointer down to put Valley Falls out in front 17-14. That was the final score. Valley Falls had won three straight, chiefly on the strength of Chip Hilton's kicking.

Chip thought about Tug Rankin a lot that night. Tug was no terminator in carrying the ball or kicking or passing, but he sure was a rugged blocker. Chip had heard the crash clear over on the sidelines when Rankin had taken out the big Stratford tackle on those two long marches. Rankin was strong. He'd found that out. Rankin was as hard as steel.

It was midseason, and the antagonism between Stewart and Brasher had just about reached the breaking point. The two men seldom spoke, even in the coaches dressing room they shared. But after the Stratford game, Stewart broke the silence.

"Look, Brasher," Chet said firmly, "these kids aren't used to the kind of talk you gave between halves today."

"So?" Brasher snarled. "Let me tell you something, my friend, you take care of your business, and I'll take care of mine. Get it?"

Stewart shook his head. "No," he said slowly, "I don't get it. My responsibility is to coach these players, too, don't forget. The way one coach acts usually reflects the attitude of the whole coaching staff. You're the head coach and should set the example."

"I'll set an example for you all right," Brasher growled menacingly. "Stay out of my face and keep your big mouth shut, or I'll close it! Get it?"

A PASS AND A PRAYER

Stewart looked him straight in the eye. "Maybe you will and maybe you won't."

Brasher was burning with fury, but he remembered Waters's and Davis's warnings. He had to control his temper. Besides, the kids were downstairs. He decided to bide his time. "I'll see you about this later," he said harshly.

Chet Stewart didn't want trouble with Brasher, but he'd nearly reached the limit of his endurance. He kept thinking about some of the things this so-called coach had done since he came to Valley Falls: teaching players dirty football, clipping, holding, illegal use of hands, beating the ball on plays. Chet couldn't resist one last statement.

"I'm getting tired of watching you teach the line to work on their opponents' heads. It's against the rules. Everybody in the state is going to find out about it sooner or later, and you'll break down all the good relations Rock has built up here in over twenty years."

Brasher was too angry to reply. His face was fiery red and his hands were trembling. He hastily dressed and left. He'd take this up with Stewart the first time he could catch him in a good place. "He's asking for it," Brasher muttered to himself.

Brasher's mood was ugly as he drove his car away from the high school. Davis and Waters usually picked him up, but this afternoon they had some sort of personal business. They hadn't even been to the game. "Leaving me to carry the whole load," Brasher kept muttering.

The farther Brasher drove, the angrier he became. Then, with a curse, he slowed down, drove around the block, and started back. He parked carefully and went up the long, winding gym steps and down the hall to the athletics office. Just as he'd hoped, Stewart was still there. Brasher slipped silently through the door, and before Stewart knew what was happening, he was fighting for his life. Brasher started swinging at Chet from behind. The first blow sent the smaller man crashing against the wall. Stewart never had a chance. Brasher was too strong and kept swinging away until he forced Stewart to the floor. Brasher fell on Stewart then and smashed him full in the face again and again. When he saw that Chet was practically helpless, he jumped to his feet.

"Now you know who's boss around here," he sneered savagely. "Open your mouth again and you'll get it worse. Get it?"

Stewart slowly staggered to his feet. He was beaten, but he wasn't quitting. "You'll hear a lot from me, Brasher," he said bitterly. "Don't worry about that."

"You still don't get it," Brasher grimaced. Before Stewart could move, the bigger man struck him again, knocking him down. Chet didn't have a chance to defend himself, just sat there on the floor with his back against the desk. Brasher looked at him contemptuously and then banged out of the office.

A little later, Chet got to his feet and went downstairs. His face was a mass of bruises. His mouth was cut, his nose was bleeding, and a shiner had appeared under one eye. "Fine lookin' thing," he muttered to the mirror. "What an idiot I am to let myself get trapped."

Rumors were flying all over school on Monday, but Soapy Smith knew the real story. "Petey told me," he whispered in the huddle. "Brasher was bragging down at the poolroom about how he beat up Chet. Didn't have a chance against that guy."

"You can tell Chet never quit," Speed Morris said bitterly, "or else he wouldn't be so cut up. He's no quitter."

On the field that afternoon, gossip was still traveling around the squad. When Brasher blew his whistle for the grass drill, Biggie Cohen never moved, looking across the field at Coach Stewart. He stood there a long time, even after Brasher had called his name. Biggie Cohen felt things deeply. Cruelty and injustice assaulted his spirit. His eyes filled with enmity for Tom Brasher.

Later, when Tug Rankin was running the varsity through the plays, he noted Biggie's lethargy and made the mistake of trying to stir him up. "Come on, Cohen, let's go! Get your head into football!"

Biggie swung around slowly and faced Rankin. "Look, Rankin," Biggie drawled, "the next time you talk to me like that, you'll wonder what hit you."

Rankin looked at him in amazement. "What's eating you?" he demanded. "What's with you? What did I say? Look, I'm just the quarterback."

"Then keep your remarks to me about quarterbacking," Biggie said, brushing past the burly quarterback.

Rankin was bewildered. "What's the matter with him?" he muttered. "What's the matter with all these guys? Doesn't anybody want to play football?"

Tug Rankin was clever. He wanted to be their leader, to build up a following in a slow but sure manner, something like Brasher had been doing, so he swallowed hard and said nothing.

Rankin wasn't afraid of Cohen or Hilton. He was no coward. He was simply bewildered. He regarded Biggie Cohen as a big, slow-moving tackle, who might be strong but who could be easily outmaneuvered in a fight. He knew he could whip Chip Hilton. Hilton was just a big, stringy guy he could take apart any time he wanted. The more he looked at Chip, the more he wanted to cut him down to size. He'd have to show Hilton who the real leader of this team was before much longer.

CHAPTER 15

East-West All-Star

TUG RANKIN had to make good in Valley Falls; his father's job and his mother's happiness depended on his ability to play football. Tug was thankful to Tom Brasher for providing him the opportunity. He also realized that Tom Brasher's only interest in the Rankin family stemmed from Tug's ability to further Brasher's coaching career. But he was loyal to Brasher and understood the problems the acting head coach faced. He knew how the players felt about Brasher and resented their dislike of his benefactor. But most of all, he resented Chip Hilton.

Tug was an ideal single-wing quarterback. His broad shoulders, thick torso, and heavy legs were built for power blocking, and he had plenty of courage. But deep down in his heart, he knew Hilton was a better all-around football player, and that knowledge ate at him. His antipathy toward the Big Reds captain grew each day until it reached jealous hate. But he was smart enough to wait, smart enough to let things ride until he got a good chance to take Hilton down.

The Southern game seemed almost like a continuation of the Stratford game to Chip. Rankin didn't use a single pass, and Southern's seven-two-two defense effectively smothered every running play the Big Reds attempted. Again and again, Chip's long punts drove the opponents back, but Southern's constant battering finally resulted in a touchdown. With two minutes left in the third quarter and with the Big Reds in possession of the ball on their own thirty, third down and sixteen, Brasher again sent Chip in to kick.

The Southerners broke through the line almost with the snap of the ball. Chip didn't have a chance to kick; he could only turn and run. He headed for the sideline, but the Southerners had every opening blocked. Then he saw Red Schwartz turn and realized Red had anticipated the punt and had looked back when it hadn't come. Chip stopped, braced his left foot sharply and hurled a pass far, far down the field ahead of Schwartz. He was immediately buried by a flock of charging Southerners, so he didn't see Red sprint after the ball and make the catch. It was one of those "Hail Mary" passes that sometimes click despite all the odds. Doug Flutie had connected on one for Boston College, and now, so had Chip Hilton.

Red caught the ball on the forty and raced all the way to the Southern six before he was downed. Chip scrambled up and sprinted after his teammates, calling, "Let's go!" He didn't glance at the sideline now but called the play on the run, skipping the huddle and going directly into the formation.

Brasher was on his feet, his face livid, but Chip wasn't aware of anything but the need to score, and he sent Cody Collins driving through left tackle on an inside reverse, plunged Badger through the middle after crossing behind Collins, and then sent Speed wide around right end for the score. It was good football and good quarterbacking.

Chip had thrown Southern off balance with the pass, and his last call had struck too swiftly for the visitors to adjust. The crowd's roar was deafening, never ceasing even when Nick Trullo spiraled the ball perfectly to Speed, who expertly placed it on the turf a split second before Chip's shoe crashed into and through the ball. But the boom of the big bass drum from the Big Reds side of the field seemed to carry above the roar as the ball soared between the uprights to put the Big Reds ahead 7-6.

Chip turned and started back up the field, glancing apprehensively toward the bench, wondering if he'd incurred Brasher's wrath again. He had! Rankin hustled out on the field. Brasher was bellowing and strode to meet Chip.

"So it was all an act! You meant to double-cross me all along, didn't you, Hilton?" Brasher raged. "Well, you'll never do it again! This time you're through for good! Get out of here before I tear that jersey right off your back! Get it?"

Chip nearly lost his composure then. But another roar from the crowd drew Brasher's attention, and Chip started for the hill, watching the action on the field as he went. Biggie had tried to kick off, but the ball had squibbed off to the left just as if it were a planned onside kick, and Lou Mazotta had recovered on the Southern forty-eight.

Chip stood by the door watching the game until the end, although there was no more scoring. But he saw that something was happening among the Big

Reds because there was a scramble and a time-out, and Brasher went out on the field. But Chip didn't find out until that evening what had really happened.

Chip's banishment had a negative effect on Tug Rankin. The husky player had been made acting captain, and it went to his head. He became another Tom Brasher, assuming the toughness and bluster during the game.

He raged from one end of the line to the other, pounding players on the back, telling them to fight, and putting on a great show. Then he made a mistake. He booted Red Schwartz in the butt. Red didn't stand for that. He straightened up from his position and kicked Rankin right back in the same spot. That did it. Rankin immediately called time and turned on Schwartz. But the official had seen the whole thing, knew a fight was brewing, and stepped between the two teammates. Brasher came out on the field and sent Schwartz to the bench. Then he sent Hill in for the redhead and gave Schwartz a tongue-lashing. The irate coach told him he'd sit the bench until he realized there had to be someone on the field to lead the team. "And that someone," he grated angrily, "is gonna be Tug Rankin! And you'll like it or else!"

While this was happening, Rankin was mentally kicking himself. As soon as Schwartz had turned on him, Tug realized he'd made a mistake. In the defensive huddle, the cold, set faces of the Big Reds warned him that his behavior was risking everything Valley Falls meant to him. These guys were bonded together by years of friendship. Tug could feel the tension in the air, and when he met Biggie Cohen's glittering black eyes, he dropped his own and quickly called for a six-two-two-one defense. Back in the safety position, he resolved to watch his step and leave all the Big Reds alone except Hilton. Later, when the Big

Reds got the ball and just before he ducked into the huddle, Tug heard Morris mutter to Cohen, "Maybe that's a good way for all of us to get on Chip's team."

Chip was only half-dressed when his teammates piled through the door. He measured their emotions, certain it would take all his leadership to keep them from walking out. He wasn't surprised when Biggie, Speed, Red, and Soapy threw themselves down with disgust on the bench in front of their lockers.

"That does it!" Schwartz said angrily. "I can't take any more of this!"

"Me," Soapy declared loudly, "I'm takin' up Rollerbladin'!"

"That goes double," Speed said grimly, glaring at Chip as if inviting an argument.

Biggie Cohen was coldly silent. He removed his shoes and his uniform with exaggerated precision, then banged everything down in the bottom of the locker. That wasn't like Biggie. He was always neat and in control. Pop Brown knew there was something wrong and tried to kid with the players, but he soon realized it was impossible.

Chip was afraid they'd quit, tell Brasher how they felt, and walk out. He breathed a sigh of relief when they all climbed into Speed's Mustang a few minutes later.

The saying "It's always darkest just before the dawn" applied to the events that night. Chet Stewart came swinging into the Sugar Bowl around seven o' clock and found Chip in the storeroom.

"Hi ya, Chipper," he said happily. "I've got some good news for you."

Chip smiled. "Coach Brasher letting me back on the team?" he asked hopefully.

A PASS AND A PRAYER

"Oh, that doesn't mean anything," Chet said sympathetically. "Don't worry about it! This is something else, something big! Something you've never experienced before! Take a guess!"

"No idea," Chip said. "I give up! What is it?"

"Well," Chet said slowly, drawing a letter out of his pocket, "right here I have an invitation for one William Hilton to appear in the East-West All-Star Game! What do you think of that?"

Chip was bewildered. "East-West game? No way!"

"Oh, yes way!" Stewart said happily. "They've invited the best football player in the state to take part in the East-West game on Thanksgiving Day in Columbus, Ohio. Now what do you think of that?"

Chip shook his head. "It's an honor, but—but I can't go. Not after being thrown off the team. It wouldn't be fair to Biggie and Speed and some of the other guys. No, one of them ought to go."

"Perhaps they should, but they haven't been invited. You have! That means every coach in the state voted for you. You were a *unanimous* selection. Think of that, unanimous! One player from each state, and he has to be a unanimous selection."

"I don't think Coach Brasher or Mr. Zimmerman would excuse me to go."

"That's all taken care of. Zimmerman knows, and he's already released it to the papers. Your mom knows too. They're tickled to death for you."

The press release wasn't really necessary. Chet Stewart had told Soapy the good news earlier, and everyone in town already knew all about it. That night Chip's friends walked home with him after work.

"Imagine," Soapy was saying, "he doesn't think he ought to go! Me? I'd start right now!"

"Me too!" Speed said. "You crazy, Chipper?"

"No, I'm not crazy," Chip shook his head. "I just don't think I ought to go. It doesn't feel right."

Biggie threw a heavy arm around Chip's shoulder. "Look, Chip" he said, "this is one of the biggest football honors that ever came to this town. It means a lot to the football fans. You've got to go! It means a lot to us too."

Mary Hilton had been watching for Chip and met him and his friends at the front door. Her first words showed how she felt about it. "Isn't it great, Chip?" She hugged him happily.

"Let's celebrate," Soapy suggested. "Is there something befitting this special, mundane—I mean momentous—occasion in the Hilton refrigerator?"

The Hilton refrigerator had something in it, all right—Chip's favorite, a huge chocolate cake. Soapy seemed to like it too. He disposed of three glasses of milk and three pieces of cake. Then he leaned back in his chair and announced to the world that he felt like a million bucks. "I could almost kiss Brasher!" he said contentedly.

There was a long silence. Soapy knew he'd messed up just as soon as the words left his mouth, and he banged his fist in despair on the arm of his chair. "I—I'm sorry. I spoiled the evening, I guess," he said morosely.

"You sure did!" Biggie said. "Well, let's go home."

"Wait a minute, guys," Chip pleaded. "While we're here, let's set it straight about the team. This makes everything all right, doesn't it?"

"It doesn't make things right about Brasher," Biggie said decisively. "Frankly, we're pretty much fed up with him, Tug Rankin, and the whole deal."

Chip argued, "You guys promised to stick it out until the Rock got better."

"We'll talk about it tomorrow," Speed said firmly.

A PASS AND A PRAYER

Chip went to bed that night with mixed emotions. He was worried about the team quitting, but he was happy he'd been selected to participate in the East-West game. It was a real honor. Only one other player in the history of Valley Falls High School football had ever achieved that distinction besides himself—his father, Big Chip Hilton.

First thing in the morning, Chip hurried out on the front porch to get the papers. He wanted to see what Waters said about the all-star game. He read the *Post* first.

LOCAL STAR TO PARTICIPATE
IN EAST-WEST GAME

Chip Hilton, outstanding athlete, has been selected to represent the state in the East-West All-Star Game in Columbus, Ohio, on Thanksgiving Day.

I've long considered Chip Hilton the most outstanding high school football player in the country. The youngster can do anything and everything with a football! The *Post* joins hundreds of Hilton's fans in congratulating him.

There was more, but Chip didn't read it. He opened the *Times* to Waters's column.

TIMES AND SPORTS
By Muddy Waters

A Valley Falls High School release received in this office late last evening announced that William Hilton has been selected to participate in the East-West All-Star Game to be held on Thanksgiving Day in Columbus, Ohio.

The news was unexpected because the Big Reds captain has been in trouble all year with the innovative head coach of the Valley Falls team. The selection probably was made because of Hilton's performances on the gridiron last year. It's doubtful that Coach Tom Brasher will permit him to accept the invitation because of Hilton's insubordination.

"Can you imagine that?" Chip gasped aloud. "What's the matter with him?" he exclaimed, throwing down the paper.

That afternoon, when his teammates came over, Chip found that Waters's column had done it. They were in open rebellion. He knew that nothing he could say would work any longer, but he had to try.

"Look," he said, "Chet said Rock was a lot better this morning. He might even be out of the hospital before the Delford game. October 29 is an open date, and that'll leave us three games to play under Rock. Come on, we don't want to spoil that. He wouldn't quit on us. Anyway, I'm not going to quit."

"You've already quit," Soapy said pointedly. "Remember? Brasher dropped you from the team!"

"Yes, but *I didn't quit* and *somehow* I'll be back, even if I have to make a public apology in front of the whole school. Tell you what I'll do. I'll make a promise with you. I'll accept the East-West invitation if you guys hang tough. OK?"

Soapy pulled on his chin and eyed the other three. "Hmmm," he deliberated, "sounds fair enough. What d'ya say, Biggie?"

"Could be a deal. I guess we all read Waters's column today, and it's easy to see where he got the info. I say OK, if Chip promises to accept the East-West invitation no matter what happens. No matter what Brasher does. Is it a deal, Chip?"

Chip nodded. "It's a deal," he said earnestly.

CHAPTER 16

Captain Versus Acting Captain

MONDAY AFTERNOON, Chip watched practice from a hall window. He was too far away to know what was happening, but he saw the squad huddled on the bleachers, with Brasher doing the talking. That evening at the Sugar Bowl, Soapy told him Tug Rankin had been appointed acting captain, pending Chip's return to the squad.

"Which means," Soapy moaned, "we now have two headaches to contend with."

On his way home, Chip was surprised to see Tug Rankin coming out of the front door of Mike Sorelli's. Mike had promised Rockwell that no player on a Big Reds team would ever be permitted in his poolroom, and every high school athlete in town knew the place was off-limits.

The meeting was unavoidable. Chip didn't want Rankin to know he'd seen him breaking a team rule and half-turned away. That's what attracted Rankin's attention.

CAPTAIN VERSUS ACTING CAPTAIN

Tug recognized Chip and stopped dead in his tracks, placing his hands on his hips, and then moved directly in Chip's path. Chip stopped short. He didn't want to stop, but he didn't intend to walk around Rankin either. Yet he was determined to avoid trouble at all costs.

"How'd practice go this afternoon, Tug?" Chip asked pleasantly. Rankin never moved or spoke a word. Chip tried again. "What's up, Tug? Are you mad at me?"

Rankin moved forward slightly. "No, I'm not mad at you, Hilton," he said brusquely. "Why should I be? You don't mean anything to me! Except that I think we've got a pretty good team, now that you're off it!"

Chip's cheeks reddened. He knew the burly quarter-back was trying to provoke a fight. But Chip didn't intend to get into a fight and add to his troubles.

"Could be," Chip said lightly. "I guess that's what Coach Brasher thinks anyway. Oh, by the way, Tug, and it's none of my business, but athletes aren't allowed in Sorelli's. Maybe no one ever told you, but that's one of the few rules the Rock won't—"

"What do I care about Rockwell?" Rankin demanded. His voice was even and his eyes were calm, but his tensed jaw muscles and hunched shoulders said he was preparing for action.

"Look, Hilton," he continued, "I go where I want. I don't know Rockwell, never saw him in my life. But if I want to hang out in Sorelli's, it's none of your business and none of Rockwell's. Understand?"

"Sure, Tug," Chip said calmly. "I don't want you to get in trouble with the coach, that's all."

"Brasher's my coach, Hilton," Rankin said angrily. "When he tells me to stay out, I'll do it. Not before!"

"Sure, Tug," Chip said slowly. "I guess you've got a right to be upset with me. Maybe I'm being nosy. Anyway,

I wish you the best of luck. By the way, I think you should know that some of the players on the team are thinking about dropping football."

"You mean your buddies want to quit, don't you, Hilton?" Tug sneered. "You mean they're like you? Won't play if they can't be the stars!"

Chip walked carefully around Rankin. "No, that isn't what I mean, Tug," he said. "I guess you just don't *want* to understand what I mean. Good night."

Tug stood frozen after Chip had left, puzzled about the reference to the team but sure now that Chip was a coward. "He's afraid of me," he muttered. "Why didn't I let him have it? He didn't have his gang with him! That's it, he won't fight unless his backup's with him. That's good to know."

At home, Tug told his father about the encounter with Chip and what Chip had said about the team. "It may be true, too, Dad," Tug said thoughtfully. "I've noticed how the players feel about Tom. I'm not too sure they understand him. In fact, I'm not too sure I understand him, but I don't want him to have any trouble. He's tough, and maybe that's the reason they don't like him."

His father interrupted him. "I know, Tug. I've been worried too. People know I'm your father, and they talk to me a lot about the team. Lots of them think Tom's arrogant and often too rough on you players. I've heard a lot of talk about the team staging a walkout. Maybe he ought to know about that. Another thing, this Hilton kid—the one you've been talking about—he's a great athlete, Tug. I've seen all the games, and you're my son, but frankly, I wouldn't say you're better. Seems too bad you both can't play; you'd make a great pair.

"Wait a minute. Don't get excited! I know you can block and you can tackle and that you've had a lot of experience in the single-wing formation, whatever that means, but you can't run, kick, or throw a ball like Hilton."

Tug's cheeks flamed and a fierce resentment was building in his chest, but he listened. He respected his father deeply and knew he was a fair and just man.

"Don't get me wrong, Tug," his father continued, "I think you're a great player too. Isn't there some way you two could work together, be friends?"

Tug squared his jaw and shook his head. "I don't think so, Dad. I'm sure Hilton's responsible for a lot of Tom's trouble, and I don't want him as a friend. Not the way I feel."

"Well, that could be, Tug, but don't forget he's the captain of the team. His teammates must respect him if they elected him captain. Seems he's pretty much a hero in this town. Maybe we both ought to talk to Tom. Why don't we do it now? Come on. Let's do it!"

While Tug and his father were driving to Tom Brasher's condo, Tom was seated in Jerry Davis's study with Muddy Waters. Brasher's sour expression clearly indicated he wasn't pleased with the conversation.

"You see, Tom," Muddy said patiently, "you're putting yourself into a corner because you won't ease up on Hilton. I'm in a position to hear these things; you're not. The people won't say to you what they say to me."

"That's right, Tom," Jerry added. "Everywhere I go I hear the same thing. Everyone says you're too tough, ride Hilton too much. Why don't you let up for a while? What do we care about Hilton? We're after Rockwell's job. Hilton doesn't mean anything; he's graduating next spring."

"Right!" Waters said. "Rockwell's the target! He's the guy we're after, and we'll get him if you'll just pay attention. People in town like the progress you've been making with the team, in spite of the low scores. Only thing I'm worried about is the kids on the team. You've got 'em down on you for some reason."

Davis nodded. "That's right! I heard my younger brother talking, and he was saying some of the regulars are ready to quit. Why don't you butter them up a bit and lay off Hilton? Let Muddy work on him in the paper. OK?"

Brasher was in a bad mood when Waters dropped him off, but he brightened up when he saw Tug and his father waiting for him.

"Hello, Tom," John Rankin said pleasantly. "I hope you won't misunderstand Tug and me, but we've been talking things over. We thought maybe there were some things you didn't know that we've been able to learn. A lot of people in town think you're doing a good job, but they're worried about your trouble with Hilton. You know, he's a favorite around this town, just as his dad was. The fans have watched him grow up, and they know what kind of kid he is."

"I know what kind of kid he is too," Brasher said shortly. "He's no good! He's been cutting my throat ever since I took charge of the team and put Tug in the quarterback slot."

"Don't get me wrong, Tom," Rankin said. "I don't want to be butting into your business, but you got me this job and you've put Tug back in school, and we're so happy here we want to do everything we can to show our appreciation."

Tug nodded his head. "That's right, Coach! I guess a lot of your trouble is because of me, putting me in at quarter and as acting captain. I'm a better football player than Hilton, Coach, don't you think?" he asked anxiously.

"You sure are!" Brasher said angrily. "Who says you're not?"

CRPTRIN VERSUS RCTING CRPTRIN

"Well, Tom," John Rankin said carefully, "I think Hilton is a—I don't know too much about styles of play and all those things—but I think Hilton is a good player, and I wish he and Tug could get along and play side by side. They'd be a great combination."

"He'll never play first string for me," Brasher said, almost shouting. "Sure, he's a good player, only he doesn't know how to control himself, wants to be the coach and everything else. Nothin' doin'! Tug's my quarterback, and he's gonna be my quarterback, and if Hilton doesn't like it, he can lump it and so can the rest of this town."

After they left, Brasher sat on the patio until late in the night. He was confused and troubled despite his confident appearance. His one ambition was to be the head football coach of Valley Falls High School; that was uppermost in his mind at all times.

Brasher was the kind of man who could never bypass something that blocked his immediate progress. In his mind, Chip was the obstruction and had to be broken. That was why there had been such a growing resentment in his heart toward Chip. But the advice he'd received this evening and the antagonism he'd sensed at practice deeply concerned him. Later, when he went to bed, they were the reasons why he couldn't sleep, why he tossed and turned all night.

Zimmerman dreaded going to his office. If it wasn't the mayor, it was the football mess or some demanding parent who wanted one of the teachers fired. Yesterday had been "Chip Hilton Day." It seemed that every sports fan in Valley Falls wanted to know why a player would be dropped from the squad because he made the play that won the game. "Discipline can go too far," one angry caller had declared.

A PASS AND A PRAYER

Zimmerman sat looking out the window, thinking of the unfortunate day that had brought him to Valley Falls. This was the only school he'd ever known in which politics governed every move a person made. He was completely dominated by the mayor and ashamed of the weakness he had shown in dealing with Tom Brasher and Tug Rankin. Of course, Condon had said he'd accept full responsibility for admitting the student and permitting him to play football, but that didn't excuse his own action.

Then there had been the appointment of Brasher as acting coach, advancing him over Chet Stewart, who was in line for the responsibility and whom Rockwell had actually designated. How'd he ever let the mayor get him in this position? He'd done little things at first to please the town's chief executive, but they were rebounding now. Little things kept getting bigger and bigger! Now he was little more than a yes-man.

He groaned inwardly when his secretary said Mr. Brasher was there to see him. "I'll see him in five minutes," he said gently and busied himself at his desk.

Brasher welcomed the brief delay. He wanted to be sure to get off on the right foot with Zimmerman. He'd spent the night worrying about the team's possible rebellion and losing the head job.

Fiery anger raced through him whenever he thought of Chip Hilton. The warnings of Tug and John Rankin, Muddy Waters, and Jerry Davis had alarmed him, and he'd decided to go easy on Hilton. He'd decided his advisers were partly right. If the team walked out, then he'd really be in a spot. He didn't have too many friends in this town as it was. This was all that Hilton kid's fault, but he was the coach and big enough to handle it.

When Brasher walked into Zimmerman's office five

minutes later, he had his plan of action clearly outlined. He surprised Zimmerman at the very beginning by jumping right into his plan.

"I believe I've been a little too hard on Chip Hilton, Mr. Zimmerman. I've been thinking it over, and I wish you'd help me try to eliminate the hard feelings that have developed between us."

Zimmerman could scarcely believe his ears. He was taken by surprise, and it took him several seconds to get over the shock. What was this all about?

"Why, Coach, I think we can do something. Naturally, when a student gets out of line, it's a disciplinary matter and we have to take the proper steps. I read your report on the latest difficulty. Just a second, I'll have my secretary bring it in."

Zimmerman pressed the buzzer and asked for William Hilton's folder. While he waited, his brain was working furiously on this new angle. What had caused this sudden change? Something was up.

Brasher's voice interrupted his thoughts. "Hilton's rather impetuous, you know, Zim, and I'm a little quick on the trigger sometimes, so I guess it's not entirely the kid's fault. I'd like to have him back."

The secretary came in at that moment, and Zimmerman welcomed the interruption. It gave him time to collect his thoughts. He opened the folder and focused his eyes on Brasher's report. But nothing registered. He was thinking as he pretended to read.

Brasher was desperate now. He didn't want this to be a long, drawn-out affair. If he could only maneuver this hardhead into bringing Hilton into the office, he could clear it up himself.

"This is Hilton's second offense, Coach," Zimmerman deliberated. "He's got to be disciplined."

"But I need him," Brasher pleaded, "and the team needs him. I'd like to take him to Weston Saturday."

"I couldn't reinstate him just like that, Tom." Zimmerman snapped his fingers. "This is the second time he's stepped out of line in two weeks."

"But couldn't you get him in here and set a limit on his team suspension? Say, two, three days?"

Zimmerman swung his chair around so he could look out the window. He didn't get it. This didn't ring true. Why should Brasher's attitude toward Hilton change so suddenly? There was something more here than met the eye. He'd call Chip in and watch their reactions. He swung back in his chair.

"That wouldn't be much of a punishment, Tom. I'll send for him. Maybe we can come to some sort of decision."

Chip knew the summons had something to do with his suspension on the previous Saturday, and as soon as he opened the door, he realized it was serious. Zimmerman's face was set in stern lines and his attitude was coldly formal. Maybe the principal was going to suspend him from school. He looked at Zimmerman with apprehension.

"Sit down," Zimmerman said sternly, nodding toward a chair by the desk. He waited until Chip was settled and then continued. "Chip, Coach Brasher reported last Saturday's incident, and I'd like to get your side of the story. I can't understand why you persist in disobeying instructions."

"Well, Mr. Zimmerman, I do try to follow them, and I didn't disobey Coach Brasher deliberately Saturday because I fully intended to kick. But I didn't have time. The Southern line was right on top of me, and I had to run. It was the only thing I could do. Then, when I saw I couldn't get away, I just threw the ball and hoped Red would catch it."

"What if Southern had intercepted the pass?" Brasher demanded. "What if they had scored on the play? We all know it would have meant defeat, and just because you didn't follow orders. Remember, it was only the third down, and you still could've kicked on the fourth down. That's why I got upset. You didn't follow orders, and it could have meant the loss of the game. But it's all over, and I'm sorry I was so hasty."

Zimmerman looked from Brasher to Chip and back to Brasher. "What do you have in mind, Coach? Do you want Hilton to apologize before the team or something? Is that what you have in mind?"

"Oh, no," Brasher said hastily, "that's not necessary. I just want Hilton to promise to follow my directions."

"Well, what about it, Chip?" Zimmerman asked, swinging his chair around so he could look into Chip's eyes. "What about following instructions?"

"I've never yet meant not to follow them, Mr. Zimmerman. I'm sorry it happened Saturday, and I'm sorry it happened the other time."

"Well, Coach, suppose I give Hilton two weeks suspension from the team and then let him come back. Let me see now, two weeks would be—ah, well, that would make him eligible for the Delford game on November 5."

"Why, that seems a little too stiff a penalty, Zim—I mean Mr. Zimmerman. I'd like to have him with us this Saturday. That's away you know, and they've got a pretty tough team."

But Zimmerman was obdurate. "No, I couldn't do that. Every student in school knows about this, and if I let him go back to the team, it wouldn't be right."

While Zimmerman and Brasher were talking, Chip was trying to understand what was behind Brasher's sudden change in attitude. "Brasher must know about the walkout," he said to himself. Then he was ashamed of his suspicions. Maybe that wasn't it at all. Yet, his knowledge of Brasher's true character warned him. No, Brasher was up to something. Whatever it was, Chip wasn't interested. All he wanted was the Rock back on the job and himself back in uniform.

"Well," Zimmerman concluded, "Chip will be eligible for the Delford game. That's the best I can do. He'll miss the Weston game, but he'll still be able to play in the Delford, Hampton, and Steeltown games. That is, if he is amenable to directions." He smiled then at Chip, and Chip's heart lifted.

"Well," Brasher demurred, "I still think it's a little too drastic, but if that's the best you can do, all right."

Zimmerman watched intently as Brasher and Chip rose, and he noted neither offered to shake hands. *There's something wrong here*, he thought to himself. "Something's definitely wrong. Brasher's completely out of character. He holds a grudge." But the discouraged principal was glad the problem was settled. He was tired of trouble.

CHAPTER 17

Today a Hero, Tomorrow a Memory

CHIP COULDN'T get Tom Brasher out of his mind. He couldn't understand the sudden reversal and show of friendship. Why would a man change so suddenly? It just didn't ring true. Chip made up his mind to accept every offer of good will but to be careful. He couldn't help distrusting Brasher. On Friday, Brasher stopped Chip in the hall and asked if he'd like to go to Weston with the team.

"I was just talking to the principal, Chip," Brasher said awkwardly. "He's agreed to let you go and sit on the bench."

Chip shook his head. "I don't think I should go, Coach, if you don't mind. Mom's got a lot of work for me to do at home, and it'll be my last chance since I'm coming back to practice on Monday."

Chip did work on the house Saturday morning, but his ear was glued to the radio in the afternoon when the Big Reds took the field against Weston. He was glad he hadn't gone with the team. It was a massacre. It was raining, but the Big Reds marched up and down the field at will. Stan Gomez just couldn't keep up with the action. Rankin was the big star, and his name came over the air time after time.

"So that cleans it up, folks, and the score: 65-0. Let me repeat that for you late listeners. The score: Valley Falls 65, Weston 0. The Big Reds were perfect this afternoon in every stat except kicking. Naturally, they didn't need it this afternoon because Weston was outclassed.

"The star of this contest, if any Big Red could be given special recognition, would have to be Tug Rankin. The big quarterback blocked with authority and played defense like a madman.

"This Big Reds team shapes up as one of the strongest in history, if not the strongest. With Chip Hilton due back in action next week, Coach Brasher will have the answer to the only weakness this team showed in its blowout victory this afternoon, the inability of anyone in the lineup to kick and pass.

"Hilton is the best kicker in high school football, and his passing is superb. If Coach Brasher can work both players into the lineup, the Big Reds will be a team of destiny, a team without a weakness. Now for some statistics—"

That night Chip could sense the pride the town was beginning to feel in the Big Reds football team and its new coach. Brasher was catching on. He was young, successful, and a bit flashy, and, more importantly to the fans, Valley Falls had won 65-0.

Football fans are peculiar; they have short memories. They usually forget the man who laid the groundwork when a successor comes along and basks in the success. Valley Falls fans were the same. They forgot this was practically the same team that had won the state championship the year before, and Henry Rockwell had put it together, had been its inspiration. The old saying "Today a hero, tomorrow a memory" is hard to believe but, unfortunately, all too often true.

"Some team, eh?" Petey voiced enthusiastically. "How about that score? Wow! There'll be a celebration tomorrow. We'll be packed!"

Chip nodded and smiled automatically, but he couldn't get the sixty-five points out of his mind. Weston must feel terrible. What an awful humiliation. Maybe the guys couldn't help it, but Brasher could have done something about it. He didn't have to keep the first string in there until the last minute of the game. Especially when the Big Reds had a lot of guys riding the bench who needed experience.

Chip's thoughts were reflected in Pete Williams's column the next day. It seemed as though the ink had been transcribed from Chip's thoughts.

VALLEY FALLS TROUNCES WESTON
BIG REDS RUN UP RECORD SCORE

Yesterday's 65-0 score may look good to the home fans, but how about the Weston fans? How about the Weston players? Why was it necessary for the Big Reds to run up the score? I've never believed that high-pressure football is necessary. The score would have been not more than half the final total if the Valley Falls reserves had been used throughout the unequal contest.

It was obvious that Weston was outclassed after the first quarter, when Valley Falls was ahead 18-0. How about the coach of the losing team? How must he feel? Don't forget most fans like to see winners! You can just imagine what the Weston fans are saying about their coach tonight.

A PASS AND A PRAYER

"Times and Sports" by Muddy Waters was a lot different. Chip read the story all the way through, but he knew what to expect without even glancing at the paper. It was Brasher and Rankin, Rankin and Brasher time after time all through the story. What else could Chip expect? Waters and Brasher were friends. Wait. Chip was getting out of line. He was thinking thoughts he shouldn't think.

Then Chip saw the other story. He looked at it with disbelieving eyes.

HILTON INELIGIBLE FOR
EAST-WEST GAME

William "Chip" Hilton, recently announced as one of the players chosen to appear in the East-West game on Thanksgiving Day in Columbus, Ohio, is ineligible according to a state rule that says the coach must attest his recommendation to that of the principal of the high school and the parents. Coach Brasher stated yesterday he had not yet given his permission for Hilton to appear in the game and, in fact, had never been asked for his recommendation.

According to the State Athletic Association rules, a player who is ineligible because of his studies or team insubordination is also ineligible for honors or postseason play. That bit of legislation cancels Hilton's eligibility, for he is, at this very minute, under suspension for insubordination.

I'm going on record as sponsoring Tug Rankin for the honor.

Chip dropped the paper as if it were red-hot. Why read the *Times* at all? Every time he picked up the paper, he saw something that portrayed him in a bad light.

Chip wasn't the only one concerned about the article.

Surprisingly, Tom Brasher was too. But Brasher meant to do something about it; he headed straight for Muddy Waters's apartment.

"Hey, Muddy," he challenged irritably. "You ask me to lay off Hilton, but you cut him to pieces and make me the bad guy. What's the deal? What's all this trash about Rankin and the East-West game?"

"What's the matter with you?" Waters demanded. "I thought you wanted me to plug Rankin."

Waters knew Brasher, knew when he was evading something. "What's it all about, Tom?" he quizzed. "What's up? You holding something back from me?"

"'Course not! But you're the guy that wanted me to get Hilton back in line, and now you're tryin' to stir up more trouble for me!"

"Look, Tom," Waters explained carefully, "what I do in the paper is a lot different than what you do on the field. A paper is an impersonal thing. But when you do something out on the field to kids, well, that upsets them, and they won't forget it."

"OK, but I don't want any more talk about Tug and the East-West game. In the first place, he isn't eligible, and in the second place, I don't want him to go. In the third place, I told Zimmerman yesterday Hilton had my approval to play!"

"What did you do that for?" Waters demanded.

"Because I couldn't stop it. This thing has been in the works a long time, before the season started. Rockwell must've worked it out. Anyone could figure that out."

"Maybe, but I've discovered most people believe what they read more than what they hear."

"Hilton's playin' in the East-West game and that's that! Stay away from that angle!"

Muddy relented. "OK, if that's the way you want it."

A PASS AND A PRAYER

The Sugar Bowl was buzzing that night. Everybody was talking about the Big Reds repeating as state champs and about an undefeated season. Little by little, the enthusiasm and thrill of success gripped the varsity.

"We're on our way," Soapy said gleefully, "on our way—Brasher or no Brasher!"

Biggie Cohen was skeptical. "I wouldn't be too sure," he said. "Look at Steeltown. They've won five in a row and haven't been held under forty points."

"That's right," Speed agreed. "You're not going to beat those babies unless you can open 'em up with some passes. Their line's as big as ours and they're good. You've got to throw a few to open up that line. Remember last year. Otherwise, our ground attack is gonna be worthless."

"They throw passes," Schwartz said gloomily. "Next to Chip, Minor is about the best passer in the state."

"Nobody can pass like Chip," Soapy proclaimed.

"Brasher better let Chip do some passin' in the Steelers game, or we'll get our butts beat," Biggie declared.

"Don't worry," Chip said optimistically, "Rock's coming along fine. He'll be back for the Steeltown game. But we've got other games ahead of the Iron Men. There's Delford and Hampton to think about first, and they're both tough. Especially Delford. You know how it is when we go there. It's a battle to the last play."

Tom Brasher knew all about Delford. His first words at Monday's practice warned that he was anticipating a rough game. But it wasn't his attitude toward the game that held his listeners' attention; it was the change in the man himself. Brasher actually smiled and joked a little. Then he grew serious.

"Hilton's back on the squad and will be able to play in the Delford game. I've also given my approval for him to play in the East-West game. Now, Delford's been here scouting every game we've played, and I think I saw a couple of their scouts at some of our away games. So I've worked up some new plays, and I want you to come back here tomorrow night knowing them. Now we'll have some group work and some pass defense, then call it a day."

Going up the hill after practice, Soapy glanced from one teammate to the other. "What's that guy think we are, computers? How we gonna memorize all these plays between now and tomorrow? He ain't human!"

"We'd better learn them," Chip said firmly. "Delford's tough, and they'd rather beat us than win the state championship."

Chip had made up his mind to continue to give Tom Brasher everything he had, but all the time he was wishing the Rock were back on the sidelines. Somehow, Brasher's change of character made Chip feel uneasy.

CHAPTER 18

Empty-Stadium Battle

TUG RANKIN was in a foul mood that night. He couldn't believe Brasher had changed his attitude about Chip Hilton so suddenly. "He acted like he was actually glad to see him back," Tug told his father.

John Rankin smiled thankfully. He hadn't noticed the bitterness in Tug's voice, and he was thinking his talk to Brasher hadn't been in vain after all. "How did the other players react to Hilton's return?"

"His friends, you mean," Tug said sarcastically. "What do you think? They acted like the guy had just won the championship all by himself."

"They say that's what he did last year, Tug. You bothered about something? Things go OK in practice?"

Tug's sour expression vanished. "Everything's fine, Dad, everything. Tom gave us some new plays and seems worried about Delford. Guess I'd better learn 'em. See you in the morning."

EMPTY-STADIUM BATTLE

Most of John Rankin's life had been a struggle. He often found it difficult to provide for his family. But he'd been blessed with a wife and son who appreciated his love and thoughtfulness. The frequent hardships had forged a strong family.

Tug worshiped his father and, more than anything in the world, wanted him to be happy. That was the reason Tug was angry at himself after he had gone upstairs to his room.

He tried to study the plays but couldn't get his mind off Brasher and Chip Hilton. "What's the matter with me?" he growled. "Why do I flip out every time someone mentions Hilton?"

Four hours later, Tug pushed his chair back from his desk and glanced at the clock. "Eleven-fifteen," he muttered. "Maybe I can settle this thing tonight." He put on his jacket and tiptoed down the stairs and out the door.

Just about that time, Chip and Petey Jackson were closing the Sugar Bowl for the night. Chip was beat, but Petey was in a hurry to get to Sorelli's to shoot a few racks before going home. Chip had to stretch out to match Petey's pace along Main Street. As Petey ducked into Sorelli's, Chip slowed and walked toward Beech Street, anticipating his comfortable bed. The Big Reds captain and the acting captain met at the corner of Main and Ninth, three blocks from Ohlsen Stadium.

Just as Chip turned the corner, Tug stepped from the shadows. "Got a minute, Hilton?"

Chip was startled, and he stopped short, his heart pounding. Then he recognized Rankin. "Oh! Sure, Tug. You scared me to death."

"That's what I figured," Tug sneered contemptuously. "You scare easy, don't you?"

"I was half-asleep."

"Maybe you were asleep Saturday afternoon when we swamped Weston without the great Hilton?"

Chip caught the antagonism in Tug's voice and instinctively braced himself.

"No, I wasn't asleep, Tug. I listened to the game on the radio."

"Well, what did you think of it?"

"I thought you guys were great, but it must have been tough for the Weston team."

Rankin grunted contemptuously. He was sure Chip was backing down. "Why don't you say what you're really thinkin', Hilton?" he demanded. "Why don't you admit you're jealous because I beat you out for the quarterback job?"

"No, Tug," Chip shook his head, choosing his words carefully. "You're wrong. I'm not jealous of you, and I—"

"And what?" Tug demanded aggressively.

"Nothing, except I think there's room on the team for both of us."

"There's not room for both of us the way we're goin', Hilton," Tug harangued angrily, "and you know it! Ever since I came to this town, you've been throwin' your weight around, tryin' to show me up, talkin' behind my back, puttin' me down to your friends. Why don't you say it to my face?"

"I never said anything I'm ashamed of, Tug. I never said anything behind your back. I never said anything I wouldn't say right now."

"Well, why don't you say you're willin' to settle things between you and me right now?"

"Because there's nothing to settle. You haven't done anything to me, Tug."

"I haven't? Then I'll do something! Right now!" Before Chip could move, Tug slapped him across the mouth. "How's that for something?"

Chip dropped back, and the blood rushed hot and angry through his whole body. But he kept his head, and his voice was even when he spoke. "This is crazy, Tug. I don't want any trouble with you."

"You're chicken, that's what you are! You're a mamma's boy! You don't want any trouble because you haven't got your gang along. That's it, isn't it?"

"I haven't got a gang, Tug."

"What d'ya call that Hilton A. C.? That's a gang, isn't it?"

"No, it isn't a gang!"

Tug lunged forward and again lashed his hand viciously across Chip's mouth. Chip's tongue immediately registered the salty blood taste, and he backed up again, barely able to restrain his anger.

"If you're not yellow," Tug demanded, "why don't you fight?"

"Because I don't have anything to fight about."

Rankin was sure of himself, certain Hilton was a coward. He'd made up his mind to finish things with Chip tonight. "Look, Hilton," he snarled, "if you don't go in the alley or some place to have this out, we'll settle it right here on the street."

Chip tried to walk around Rankin, but Tug moved across his path. Chip made one more try to avoid the fight. "Why don't we settle this at the Y, Tug? With gloves!"

"With gloves?" Tug echoed sarcastically. "Now wouldn't that be divine? You and your gang in the Y. Not a chance! We'll go in the alley! *Now!*"

"No," Chip said, "that would be just as bad. Come on, Tug, why should we act like little kids, fighting over nothing?"

"You want to chicken out of it, that's what's the matter with you," Rankin retorted angrily.

"No, Tug," Chip said quietly. "I'm not trying to chicken out of anything. It just seems, well—"

"It doesn't seem anything 'cept you're yellow!"

"All right, Tug," Chip sighed resignedly, "if there's no way out, I guess I'll have to fight. How about the stadium?"

"Suits me."

Side by side, they matched strides, walking swiftly up the street to the high school, across the broad lawn, up the steps to the gym, and along the fence to the gate. Without a word, they climbed over and dropped to the ground. The only sound in the stadium was the soft padding of their shoes on the grass. They reached the lower level, crossed the all-weather track, and headed straight for the south goal, just as if they had previously decided on that spot as the place to settle their differences. Tug shed his jacket and carefully placed it next to one of the uprights, while Chip pulled his varsity sweater over his head and laid it beside the coat.

"I still say this is silly," Chip uttered flatly.

Rankin grunted. "What's the matter, Hilton?" he growled "Gettin' cold feet?"

Chip didn't answer, and Rankin grunted again. "Now," he gritted, "we'll settle things!" It was a dark night, and the walls of the stadium left barely enough light to make out the dead whiteness of each boy's face in the pale light of the stars.

Chip could hardly see Rankin's head but sensed his shorter adversary would come in swinging with both arms. So he stood his ground, his arms hanging loosely at his sides, content to let Tug take the initiative. But he made one last effort to avoid the fight.

"Tug," he said evenly, "you're forcing me to fight. I'd still like to call it off."

EMPTY-STADIUM BATTLE

"You can't talk your way out of this, Hilton," Rankin grated. "I've been waitin' too long to corner you without your gang. I'm gonna take care of you right now!"

Then, just as Chip had expected, Rankin charged forward, swinging viciously with lefts and rights for Chip's jaw. The rush was made to order for a counterpuncher, but Chip sidestepped and spun Tug to the right. Rankin turned around and started another rush. This time, Chip moved forward, met the charge, and turned Tug to the left.

Rankin's momentum carried him several steps away before he could recover his balance. He stood still for a moment, breathing heavily. "Won't fight?" he snarled. "Well, we'll see about that."

Again Rankin came charging out of the darkness. This time he withheld his blows and, at the last instant, dove hard into Chip's legs, trying to knock him down. Chip had known from the first rush that Rankin was an inexperienced boxer. He also knew his bulky adversary was a powerful puncher and in the semidarkness might land heavily. But Chip wasn't prepared for the change in tactics and went down under Tug's weight. The fall jarred him, knocking the wind out of his lungs, and finally convinced him there was no way out except to fight on Rankin's terms. He rolled with the fall, spun out of Tug's grasp, and leaped to his feet fully determined.

Chip backtracked a few steps before Rankin's advance. Then, as Tug charged with swinging fists, Chip stepped forward and drove a straight left to the nose and followed with a hard right to Tug's jaw. It was a beautiful one-two and sent Rankin reeling back on his heels.

Rankin seemed to sense Chip was the superior boxer, for he stood there a second, snarling for Chip to "come on and fight!"

A PASS AND A PRAYER

Chip waited silently, as before, and once again Rankin charged forward. This time Chip sidestepped to the left and smashed a hard right directly into Tug's mouth. That punch had authority behind it, but it didn't stop Tug's rush, and the two boys grappled once again. Tug tried to wrestle Chip to the ground, but Chip twisted and turned and proved his superiority, rocking Rankin's head with a series of short blows. Tug broke away and came in again, swinging with both arms. Chip grasped Tug's arm and pulled him forward, then swung in behind Rankin and threw him heavily to the ground. But Chip didn't hold him there, didn't even try. He leaped up and away, and Rankin grunted with surprise as he scrambled to his feet.

Both boys labored to breathe, and Tug began to have his doubts about the vulnerability of his slender opponent. But only for a second. Once more he rushed, arms flailing, and once more Chip counterpunched straight from the shoulder, hard into Rankin's face. Then Chip gave ground, leading Tug forward.

Tug was tired and hurt, but his pride was damaged the most. His arms hung low at his sides, and as he gasped for breath, he tried to steady himself for another charge. Then, with a snort of anger, he hurled himself forward, determined to close in on Chip and wrestle him to the ground.

Chip met his lunging opponent more than halfway, driving inside Tug's grasping arms and smashing two heavy blows into Tug's face. Tug grabbed and held on, then wrestled Chip to the ground. But it was Chip who landed on top and straddled Tug's thick trunk with his long legs.

Tug tried to cover up, expecting Chip to pound away at his face, but Chip merely held his arms until Rankin ceased struggling. Then Chip got up, picked up his sweater, and walked away without a word.

Tug sat there in the stadium a long while, thoroughly whipped, and just about as sick at heart as he had ever been in his life. He couldn't believe it, and if he hadn't been so thoroughly marked up, he'd have thought it was all a bad dream.

Behind the wooden railing that separated the track from the first row of seats in the stadium, a figure, obscured by the darkness, had watched the entire fight. But the person didn't make a move until both boys left the stadium. Then he grunted with satisfaction and followed.

Pop Brown had been at Valley Falls for more years than anybody could remember, but he had never enjoyed anything as much as the battle he had just witnessed. As he followed Chip and Tug out of the empty stadium, he chuckled with glee and headed straight for Chet Stewart's house. Chet put down his coaching magazine as soon as he heard Pop's voice.

"Chipper made him say uncle, Chet—three times! Man, oh man, I sure wish you could've seen it!"

"Why didn't you let me know?"

"How could I? I didn't know there was gonna be a fight. I saw Rankin stop Chip at the corner, and I could tell by the way they were talking something was gonna happen, so I followed and watched."

"Now look, Pop," Chet admonished sternly, "that fight was the business of those two kids, and I don't want you to tell another soul about it. Understand?"

Pop nodded. He was satisfied, now that he had shared the good news with Chet. Pop knew a lot about Tom Brasher and Tug Rankin and Chet Stewart and Chip Hilton, and he knew Chet Stewart was pleased and would feel a lot better now. As he walked slowly home, he was chuckling, and he knew Chet Stewart was chuckling too.

Tug Rankin was in the bathroom a long time that night, but his eyes, nose, and mouth needed more than hot towels. He looked in the mirror and groaned. What was he going to do tomorrow? He'd be laughed at all around school, and Hilton would probably be strutting all over the place. He went over the fight in his mind. He'd sure underestimated Chip Hilton! His father had been right about Hilton all along. Why hadn't he realized it? A guy who could play football like Hilton couldn't be a coward.

Tug shook his head in wonderment. "He let me up three times," he muttered. "I wouldn't have let *him* up. Maybe I've been wrong about him!"

Tug's anguish started the next morning at breakfast. John Rankin spotted Tug's split lip, black eyes, and swollen nose as soon as Tug sat down at the table.

"What happened to you, Tug?" he asked in an alarmed voice.

"Oh, I had a little trouble, Dad."

"A little trouble? What about? Who with?"

"Chip Hilton! We had a fight!"

"A fight! Why? Did Hilton start it?"

"No, Dad, I started it, but he finished it."

"Good grief, what does he look like?"

"I guess he must look all right. I haven't even hit him yet!"

John Rankin looked at his son incredulously. "Haven't hit him yet? How many were there? What'd they do, sneak up from behind or something?"

"No, Dad, there was just Hilton. I started it, slapped him twice and called him a mamma's boy and finally baited him into fighting, and he gave me a good one. He got me down and then let me up. Let me up three times. He can fight like a wildcat, and because he didn't want to fight, I thought he was a coward."

"He isn't, Tug," John Rankin began slowly, "not at all. You know, Tug, I've been wanting to talk to you for a long time. Maybe this is just as good a time as any. I've been hoping you'd come to understand real sportsmanship. I guess you and I are a lot alike. We've had it pretty tough, and it's made us a little selfish and a little bitter. In sports, they call people like you and me competitive athletes. We compete—so does Hilton—but there's a difference all right. Other athletes want to play and win as badly as we do. But we get so wrapped up in ourselves, we forget the others. We overlook the others; he doesn't.

"I like Tom Brasher, Tug, and I know he's done a lot for us, but he's also done something to you that has me worried. Tom's set on being a success at any cost, and you're getting to be that way too. In a way I'm sorry we had to obligate ourselves to him, because now we have to go along with everything he does. I've felt all along Hilton was right and Tom was wrong. What you've just told me makes me more sure than ever Chip Hilton was right. How do you feel about him?"

"It's weird, Dad, but I never liked him until last night. I can't understand it. Guess I ought to hate his guts after last night, but somehow I don't feel so bad about him. I suppose he'll lord it all over me around school."

"No, Tug, I don't think so. I don't think he'll say a word about it. Why don't you run a little test? Keep it to yourself and see if he keeps it to himself."

CHAPTER 19

True Colors

HENRY ROCKWELL was a fighter, spiritually and emotionally. He was affectionately known as Hank by his friends and generally referred to as the Rock by the residents of Valley Falls, and the abbreviation of his surname best described his moral and physical attributes. Rockwell adamantly adhered to his principles and was stubborn in his opinions. He was a man of action, and as the long days dragged slowly into weeks of hospitalization, the four walls of his private room closed in on him a little more each day. He became restless, irritable, and a more difficult patient. He was almost impossible this particular morning when Doc Jones found him sitting up in bed, glaring at the door.

"When do I get out of this place?" Rockwell demanded.

"Now, Hank," Doc soothed, "take it easy. After all, I've been taking care of you a long time."

"Sure! You brought me into the world a hundred years ago! So what?"

"Nothing, except you have to have confidence in me. After all, when you know someone a hundred years—"

"A hundred years too long," Rockwell blustered. "What is this, a jail? When do I get out of here, Mr. Judge?"

"Now look, Hank, I promised you'd be out of here by Thanksgiving."

"You did not! You said I'd be out of here by the first of the month!"

"I didn't say what month."

"Tomorrow's the first of November and I'm leaving."

"No, you're not, Rock, because you're not well enough. Maybe in a week or another ten days it will be all right. Right now, it would be suicide."

"Ten days? That would be November 11."

"You've got it," Jones said, chuckling. "I'll even let you go to the game that afternoon, let you sit in the stands. It's the return Hampton game, and the team only won by a point over there. What do you say?"

"Will you shake hands on that?" Rockwell demanded.

"Sure!" Jones agreed. "With you? Any time!"

"Now listen, Doc," Rockwell warned, "I'm not kidding about this. I can't stand this dungeon much longer. If you don't get me released from here by November 11, I'll sign myself out!"

Valley Falls High was still pumped about the Weston score, and students gathered in small knots in the halls and outside on the steps, talking about the game. Interest shifted, with a rush, when Tug Rankin showed up with black eyes, a cut lip, and swollen nose. Word spread like wildfire that Tug Rankin had been in a fight and had taken a beating. But Rankin wasn't talking, and his belligerent attitude discouraged questions.

A PASS AND A PRAYER

Chip could feel his teammates staring at him, trying to detect some signs of a clash. He appeared fine and remained silent. Soapy couldn't take it; he was itching with curiosity. When he saw Rankin in the hallway, it was his chance to gain some relief.

"You run into a door, Rankin?" Soapy asked loudly.

"No," Tug said wryly. "I ran into a bulldozer. And I mean a bulldozer!"

Tug's reply amazed everyone. This was the first time Rankin had shown any signs of friendliness. They were even more amazed when Tug continued. "I got taught a good lesson Saturday night. Supposed to be a fixed fight. I was supposed to win, but I haven't hit the guy yet!"

Tug looked squarely across the hall at Chip, trying to catch his eye. Chip resolutely closed his locker and walked to class. Rankin's glance told the story. Everyone knew the opponent and winner had been Chip Hilton. That put the muzzle on Soapy and everyone else, and Tug Rankin's respect for Chip and his friends soared. They went out of their way to be friendly, and Tug's appreciation of good fellowship developed more and more. He began to appreciate what it meant to be "one of the guys."

Chip got a surprise that afternoon, too, because Brasher gave him a chance at quarterback on the first team. Despite Brasher's friendliness, Chip remained dubious. This new Brasher just didn't ring true. Brasher continued his campaign to win over the players by announcing they'd spend the night in Delford. The week passed quickly, and as reports of Rockwell's improvement filtered through school, team spirit percolated among the Big Reds.

When the Big Reds rolled out for Delford the next morning, they were once again the state champs, the team without a care. They checked in at the Jefferson Hotel, and after lunch Brasher gave the team free time in the afternoon. Several players stayed in their rooms to watch a college football game, but the largest group headed for the mall theater. After the movie the rest of the guys went to their rooms before Brasher's pregame meeting. But Chip stopped in the hotel gift shop. That's how he heard the conversation.

"Hey, Tug! Hey, Rankinowitz!"

Chip's head jerked around in surprise. Tug? Rankinowitz? His eyes located the speaker, an unfamiliar figure who was waving excitedly and rushing toward Tug Rankin who had just entered the lobby.

"Rankinowitz," Chip mumbled to himself. "Rankinowitz! That must be his name! Must have been abbreviated to Rankin!"

Tug's friend was husky and about Chip's age. He and Rankin were shaking hands and laughing as if they hadn't seen each other for a long time. They sat down in front of the fireplace and seemed to be discussing old times. Chip continued to his room, but the incident struck a note of something important to come.

Chip had looked forward to this game because the Big Reds were playing under the lights and because he thought Brasher might give him a chance to play offense. But the game repeated the pattern of all the others: Brasher sent him in to kick off and then replaced him with Rankin. Delford was big and fast, and the game was a standoff throughout the first half. Neither team scored.

The game broke open in the third quarter when Delford scored on a pass, made the extra point, and tallied a field goal. Valley Falls managed to punch a lonely touchdown across, failing on the two-point try by Rankin. It looked as though the scoring would end that way until Speed Morris came through with one of his last-minute clutch specialties, breaking around right end and sprinting seventy yards for a touchdown to put the Big Reds out in front, 12-10. Brasher sent Chip in to kick the point after and Chip made it 13-10. That's the way the game ended with Valley Falls winning its sixth-straight.

When Chip arrived home, he found a letter on his desk from the director of the East-West All-Star Game. The selection committee was happy he had accepted the invitation and considered it an honor to list him as one of the outstanding players who would compete. Also enclosed was the program from last year's game, containing pictures and profiles of the players and coaches.

Chip flipped on his stereo, dove on the bed, and read through the program. Chip studied the faces. Then he nearly fell off the bed! His eyes bulged, and he turned the pages rapidly until he came to the names of the West players. He found what he was looking for and then whistled softly to himself. Now he began to understand why Tug Rankin had appeared on the scene in Valley Falls!

Louise Rockwell had been through many difficult years as the wife of Henry Rockwell, but the job of keeping him in the hospital, away from his players, the games, the papers, and the television had been the most difficult task she'd ever faced. As the days slipped by, she began to dread November 11. She and Doc Jones were both aware her husband's reaction to the football situation might send him reeling into a relapse. Then, on Wednesday, she and Doc Jones got a break. Rockwell developed a slight cough.

"That settles it!" Jones said firmly. "You're not leaving this hospital. Don't argue! It's final! You can go home Sunday, pick up where you left off with the team on Monday, and by Saturday you'll be strong enough to handle the bench."

"But you said I would be all right by tomorrow. What's a little cough?"

"A little cough can be dangerous, particularly when you're in a weakened condition. It's going to be damp tomorrow, and you'll get down with that cold and have a relapse and be right back where you started. Probably wouldn't get out of here till Christmas."

"We had an agreement!"

"Please, Henry," Louise Rockwell protested. "Doc knows best."

"I won't promise," Rockwell said grudgingly. "We'll see how my cough is in the morning. If it isn't any better, I'll stay here and listen to the game. That a deal?"

Jones breathed a sigh of relief. "It's a deal!"

Doc Jones was hoping to keep Rockwell away from the football field until he was stronger. His recovery from pneumonia was taking all his energy. Doc didn't want Rock to learn about Brasher's supervision of the team or the elimination of the spin-T until the ailing coach was in good physical condition. He didn't want Rockwell to find out Chip had been benched. Louise Rockwell completely supported Doc's judgment.

On November 11, Henry and Louise Rockwell and Doc Jones were sitting in the glass-enclosed sunporch listening to the broadcast of the Valley Falls-Hampton game from Ohlsen Stadium.

Stan Gomez was at his best, interjecting personality notes and talking enthusiastically about the Big Reds. As Gomez talked, Rockwell grew puzzled.

"Rankin? We don't have anyone by the name of Rankin. Who does he mean? What's the matter with Chet? Why didn't Chet choose the starting team?" He turned to Jones. "Chet sick?"

"No," Jones deliberated, "I don't think so."

"Well, where is he? Who's running that team? What is this?"

Louise tried to quiet him. "Now, Hank, you promised to listen quietly."

Rockwell grunted. "I don't get this. Where's Chip? Why isn't he in the starting lineup? Rankin? There's no one in Valley Falls by the name of Rankin."

"Yes, there is, Rock," Jones said. "The family moved here just before school started, and the kid is quite a player."

"Can't be better than Chip!"

"No, but he's a good quarterback."

"You mean Chip rides the bench?"

Jones cast an appealing glance at Louise Rockwell. "Not exactly, Rock. I guess you'd say the two sort of share the job."

"Don't get it," Rockwell fumed. "Where did these Rankins come from?"

"I really don't know, Rock. All I know is the kid's a good quarterback."

Just then the voice of Stan Gomez cut into the conversation.

"—A high one down to Tug Rankin on the ten. Rankin is up to the fifteen, the twenty, and he's snowed under on the twenty-two. Ball is on the twenty-two, first and ten. The Big Reds are out of their huddle. Backfield to the right. There's the pass from Trullo to Morris. He's driving over right tackle. Oh! What a crash! Morris must have been hit by a truck. It's second and ten. No gain on the play. There goes Badger, number 11, over left guard. He's stopped hard at the line for no gain. Valley Falls calls time."

Rockwell was bewildered; he couldn't understand the plays. He knew his formation and plays by heart; he'd developed the tricky offense himself. Now he was trying to figure "backfield to the right" and which of his plays permitted the use of a snap from center to left half, from Trullo to Morris.

"Can't be," he muttered. "Can't be!"

"Chip Hilton in for Rankin. You won't have many more chances to see that big 44 in action, folks. The Rock told me personally before his illness he meant to retire that number permanently when Hilton hangs up his gear next June. 'Course, you haven't seen much of the all-state quarterback all year since Coach Brasher inaugurated his new offensive style of play."

Rockwell turned off the radio, turning accusing eyes on Doc and his wife.

"New offense! Coach Brasher! Tug Rankin! No wonder you've been afraid to let me listen to the games! What's become of Chet? Where's my clothes? I'm going to my room!"

Doc Jones had handled hysterical children, addicts with injuries, and half-crazed patients, but he had never met anyone like this angry football coach. In the end, he succeeded in calming his old friend, but he knew Henry Rockwell had reached the limit of his patience. Jones solemnly promised he'd release the coach Sunday evening, and that kept the angry invalid from immediately walking out of the hospital. At that point, Doc Jones couldn't stand the suspense and switched on the radio.

Early in the second half, Chip kicked a second field goal with Hampton ahead 18-6. Rankin began wishing he could get out of the game. Hampton's line had neutralized the Big Reds running attack, and Tug knew they were going down if they didn't do some passing to open up Hampton's secondary. "I'm not a passer! We need Chip," he murmured. "He ought to be in here!"

At the next time-out, Rankin walked over to the sideline. "Can I speak to you a minute, Coach?" he asked.

Brasher edged close to the sideline. "Sure, what is it?"

"I think Hilton should take over and throw some passes. They've got our running attack stopped cold."

Brasher looked at him in amazement. "Hilton? Are you nuts? Who's running this team? Get out of here! Get back in that game! What's the matter with you?"

Rankin turned away, and Brasher watched the retreating figure incredulously. "What's this all about?" he muttered. "I thought Tug hated the guy."

In his hospital room, Henry Rockwell was infuriated. He knew what was wrong with the Big Reds in the game and in other ways too. This Brasher must be insane.

"Phone down there, Doc, find out what's wrong with Chip. Get Brasher on the bench phone!" he fumed.

Jones nodded his head. "Right! I'll call!"

But Jones didn't call. He knew exactly what was wrong and had known for some time. He knew all about Brasher and Rankin and Chip, but he left the room, walked down the hall, visited another patient, and then came back. It was a good thing he did because Rockwell was half-dressed when Doc returned.

"Now wait a minute, Hank," he said. "You get right back in that bed."

"Nothing doing!" Rockwell bellowed. "I'm going to that game and no one's going to stop me!"

Doc had been holding out on Rockwell, but he took hold of him now, firmly grasping him by the arm.

"You wanna fight?" asked Rockwell, pulling free.

"Sure!" Jones laughed. "Sure, I wanna fight!"

"Me too," Louise Rockwell declared. "Let's all fight! Get the nurses too!"

They all laughed at their foolishness, and finally, Rockwell climbed back into bed and the radio blared again.

"Valley Falls has called time-out. I think Rankin is hurt. Yes, number 4, Tug Rankin, is hurt! Hilton is replacing Rankin. We'll probably see some passing now. These Big Reds better do some passing if they expect to get back in this game. Hampton leads 18-6."

But Tug Rankin wasn't hurt. He was pretending. Lying on the ground, he realized this was the only way his team could win. Chip Hilton was the answer. Chip could do it! So when he was carried off the field, he closed his eyes, not from pain, but to hide his real feelings.

Brasher was desperate. "What's the matter, Tug?" he demanded. "You have to come out?"

Rankin nodded. "Yes, Coach, it's my knee."

"Can you stand on it?"

"No, I can't!"

Tug closed his eyes. He'd been acting a lie ever since he came to Valley Falls. Now he'd lie for a good cause, for a change.

Tom Brasher looked down the bench. There was nothing he could do except replace Rankin with Hilton. He hesitated, and then he heard the crowd roar.

"We want Hilton! We want Hilton!"

"It's my own fault," Brasher muttered. "If I hadn't tackled that Connors kid at Midwestern, I wouldn't be in this mess now."

"Hilton!" he called. "In for Rankin!"

A PASS AND A PRAYER

The Big Reds suddenly caught fire under Chip's leadership and started to march down the field. Everything Chip tried clicked. He ran with the ball for consistent gains, passed to Morris or Collins in the flat, hit Schwartz for a fifteen-yard gainer down the center, blocked, and handled the ball perfectly. Three minutes after Chip's entrance into the game, the Big Reds had a touchdown and the extra point and trailed 18-13.

Brasher's true colors emerged when the Valley Falls cheerleaders began the roar for Hilton. Then, when every person in the stadium stood up and cheered Chip as he trotted up the field, Brasher lost his cool. He couldn't stand watching Hilton receiving acclaim. He suddenly decided to yank Chip out even if it meant losing the game. He rushed to Rankin's side and shook him roughly.

"Look, Tug, you gotta get in there!"

Rankin shook his head. "No, Tom, I can't stand on my leg."

"You'll have to! Stand up! Get in there! You just go in there and play! Get up! Go in there for Hilton! He's takin' all the glory of this game. He's makin' us both look bad!"

But Tug wasn't going back into that game. He had, at last, come to his senses. He knew now what kind of man Tom Brasher really was. He couldn't help comparing him with Henry Rockwell. He'd heard about Henry Rockwell even though he'd never played under him. He knew Rockwell wouldn't let an overtired or injured athlete compete. He knew from what he'd heard that the Rock would rather lose a championship than see a player get hurt. Rankin realized now there wasn't a thing about Brasher to warrant his loyalty. His dad had been right. Brasher wanted victory at any cost, even at the expense of serious injury to a player. No. Tug Rankin would never play football for Tom Brasher again.

CHAPTER 20

No Substitution

BRASHER WAS desperate. He waited until Chip kicked the ball, then grasped Bill Carroll by the shoulders, sending him in to replace Chip. The substitution immediately paid off—for Hampton. Hampton gambled, throwing a long pass, which sailed over Carroll's head and into the arms of the Hampton right end. Speed hauled him down on the thirty. Chip buried his head in his hands. There went the ball game. The crowd's roar jerked his head up, and he saw Hampton had fumbled. The fullback picked up the loose ball and tried to run, but Biggie Cohen nailed him for a ten-yard loss. Three downs later, the Hampton punter drilled a low spiral out of bounds on the Valley Falls eight-yard line.

Chip was on his feet now, watching the clock and yelling, "Come on! Come on!" Behind him, the Valley Falls stands chanted, "We want a touchdown! We want a touchdown!"

Chip glanced at the clock. There were five minutes to play, and the score remained Hampton 18, Valley Falls 13. Plenty of time if the Big Reds could get their attack moving. But Hampton meant to protect its lead, and without anyone to pass, the Big Reds couldn't gain a yard. Hampton held Valley Falls for no gain on three straight tries.

Every down spelled disaster. If Valley Falls lost this game, its goal of the sectional championship vanished. How could it be won? Maybe with a pass.

Chip didn't waste any more time. He cast one determined look at Brasher, then grabbed his helmet and dashed on the field. Brasher was bellowing at the top of his voice, but Chip paid no heed. He headed straight for the huddle. He was the captain of this team, and Rock had said he had certain responsibilities. He glanced at the clock—two minutes and fifteen seconds left to play, and fourth down coming up. Well, a team might as well be tromped 40-13 as 18-13. One point or a hundred— what did it matter? People only remembered that you won or lost.

During the fleeting seconds it took him to reach the huddle and send Bill Carroll trotting off the field, Chip had decided the play he was going to call, the fourth-down gamble he was going to take. Behind him, on the sidelines, Tom Brasher was shouting at the officials, demanding a time-out, making every effort to stop the game. But Chip had called the play, and the team was hustling to the line.

Chip dropped back into the end zone, and his teammates lined up in punt formation. "Maybe it'll work," he breathed. "It's got to work!"

Chip called the fake-punt play this time, but he tied Rockwell's flea-flicker on the end of it. He didn't shift his eyes, but he saw Red Schwartz had dropped back a yard from his end position, and Cody Collins had replaced him on the opposite side of the line. So far so good. The ball came spinning back, and Chip faked the kick, held the ball, and cut to the right, followed by half of Hampton's forward wall. But the defensive linemen changed direction and took out after Schwartz when Chip tossed over their heads to the redhead.

That freed Chip, and when Schwartz flipped the ball back to him, he had plenty of time to locate Biggie Cohen barreling down the left sideline. Chip gauged Biggie's speed and let the ball fly. It was a blind pass; Chip never saw Biggie Cohen catch it on the forty-yard line and stumble to the fifty before he went down. The tremendous roar from the stands signaled to Chip that Biggie had caught the ball. He hurried up the field, his heart jumping. The play had clicked. Hampton had called time, and Tom Brasher was out on the field hollering at the referee. "Grimes!" he called. "Grimes! I want to make a substitution!"

"Well, make it! But stay off the field!" Grimes said testily.

"Taylor!" Brasher shouted. "Taylor, take Hilton's place! Hurry!"

Jordan grabbed his helmet and started on the field, but he never reached the huddle.

"Get off the field, Hilton!" Brasher had followed Taylor out on the field. Now he turned to Grimes and Taylor. "What's goin' on here?" he yelled. "I want Hilton out of there! I sent in this sub!"

"Yes, but he wasn't recognized," Grimes said softly.

"Wasn't recognized? What do you mean, he wasn't recognized?"

"He means," Soapy wisecracked from the bench, "they haven't been properly introduced."

Brasher glared at Soapy and took a step in his direction, then turned back. "I want that player in the game, and I want Hilton out!"

A PASS AND A PRAYER

Grimes was an official of the old school. He looked at Brasher coldly. He'd heard of Brasher, but this was the first game he had worked for Valley Falls. "Maybe you ought to read up on the rules, Coach," he said coolly. "A player continues to be a player until a substitute enters the field and indicates to the player that he is replaced."

Grimes turned to Jordan. "Are you indicating to this player he is being replaced?" he asked, winking and grinning.

Jordan shook his head vigorously. "No, sir! Not at all, sir! We're perfectly happy."

"And how," Soapy echoed from his vantage point on the sideline. "And how!"

"All right, then," Grimes concluded, "time's up. Play ball! Off the field, Coach."

Brasher was beyond logical reasoning now, nearly frantic with rage. "I demand that substitution be made!"

"If you don't get off the field," the referee warned, "I'll be forced to penalize your team."

"Penalize them! See if I care!" Brasher blazed.

"All right, I will!" Grimes said coolly, picking up the ball and stepping off five yards. "That's for delaying the game."

"Penalize us again," Brasher berated.

"All right," Grimes said, stepping off five more yards, "I'll do that too!"

"Please, Mr. Grimes," Chip pleaded, "don't penalize us again. We'll be back to our own goal before he stops."

The Valley Falls fans were spilling out of the stands. They lined the field's perimeter. They knew something was wrong, and they knew the Big Reds were being penalized because Brasher refused to leave the field. Muddy Waters dashed out on the field.

"Tom," he said, pulling Brasher's arm. "Tom, you crazy fool, get off the field. What's the matter with you? Are you completely nuts?"

NO SUBSTITUTION

Waters never got a reply. Chip had called the play; the Big Reds were at the line, and Trullo was over the ball. Chip faked a pass, cut around right end, and carried the ball down to the twenty-yard line. It was a beautiful run, but Chip had only one thought. He glanced at the clock. Fifteen seconds to go.

Then Chip turned to his teammates. "Fifteen seconds to play, guys. No time for a huddle. Time for only one play. I'll try a place kick. Line up and listen! Come on, Speed, get set! Ball on three! Hold back their line!"

Chip darted back nine yards, and Morris knelt for the snap from Trullo. Then Chip gave Rockwell's audibles, the signals the team always used when time was short and the huddle was eliminated. He sure hoped the Big Reds were paying attention.

"Block that kick! Block that kick!"

The Hampton captain was smart. "He won't kick!" he yelled desperately. "Three points won't do 'em any good! Watch out! It's a pass!"

He was right, but his teammates had been fooled. They realized too late that Chip's call had been a ploy. The ball flashed through Speed's outstretched arms, and Chip cut to the right, faking toward Speed, who was cutting toward the right corner of the end zone. At the last instant, he turned, and with a perfect peg right in the numbers, he hit Red Schwartz standing on the goal line, far to the left. Red stepped across the line as time expired, and Valley Falls had won its seventh-straight. The score: Valley Falls 19, Hampton 18. The Big Reds were still undefeated, still in the running for the championship of Section Two.

Ohlsen Stadium was a madhouse. The Valley Falls fans swarmed the field. The crowd caught Chip and Schwartz and hoisted them in the air, carrying them to the gate leading up the hill to the locker room.

Chip had forgotten Brasher and everything but those last few seconds. He had closed his eyes on the fourth-down gamble. Not on the pass he had made to Red but on the one to Cohen. He turned and grasped his friend by the arm. "I *did* close my eyes on that pass to you, Biggie. I never even saw you catch the ball."

"You know, Chip," Biggie drawled, "I closed my eyes too."

Brasher hadn't been able to get near Chip after the game, but he waited upstairs in the athletics office, his angry eyes focused on the door leading to the locker room. Downstairs, Chip's teammates were throwing socks, shoes, and pads at one another and yelling jubilantly. Chip dressed and slipped up the steps, determined to escape while target practice was in full swing.

He closed the door behind him only to be hit by a tornado. Brasher grabbed Chip by the shoulders and banged him viciously against the door.

"You're through! This time for good! You'll never play another down for Valley Falls High School! You hear? You miserable traitor!"

"I didn't—"

"Shut up!" Brasher grated, striking Chip across the mouth. "I oughta smash your head in. Get outta my sight!"

Chip pushed Brasher away and walked slowly down the hall. This was not a coach! That settled it. Now, he'd act.

Half an hour later, Soapy and the team, still celebrating, arrived at the Sugar Bowl. Soapy greeted Petey Jackson with a grandiloquent wave of his hand.

"The Soapy special for everyone, my good man," he ordained. "It's on the house!"

Petey stared. "Oh, yeah," he drawled, "and since when did you buy the place? No way! Show me the money!"

NO SUBSTITUTION

Chip settled that argument by tossing some bills on the marble fountain counter. "Out of that, Petey," he smiled. Then he asked Speed to wait and dragged Soapy into the storeroom.

"Now, listen!" he commanded. "This is important!"

Thirty minutes later, Chip hurried back to the fountain, whispered something in Speed's ear, then dragged the speedster out the door and into his fastback.

"Where we goin'?" Speed demanded.

"Never mind! How's the tires?"

"Tires?" Speed echoed. "I don't need tires! Where we goin'?"

"Never mind," Chip said. "John Schroeder's first."

John Schroeder opened the door just as Chip rang the doorbell. "Saw you through the window," he explained. "What a game! What a finish! What a thriller!" John Schroeder was so enthused about the game he didn't realize until later that Chip had asked him for one hundred dollars and he'd given it to him. "Now what do you suppose Chip needed that much money for?" he muttered. "Wonder where he's going?"

Chip took the steps four at a time and vaulted into the red Mustang. "Let's go," he said.

"Where?"

"To your house to ask your parents if you can be away until Monday."

"Sure, I can be gone till Monday. But where?"

"Never mind. While you're talking to them, I'll call Mom and tell her about it! Hurry, we've got a long trip ahead of us between now and Monday."

Speed didn't know where he was going and didn't care as long as he was with his friend, Chip Hilton. But Chip Hilton knew exactly where he was going. He was on his way to clear up this Brasher matter once and for all.

CHAPTER 21

False Heroes

PETE WILLIAMS was a good sportswriter, a strong booster of high school football, and one of Chip Hilton's most enthusiastic fans. He was disgusted by Muddy Waters's persistent and unwarranted attacks on Chip in the *Times* all through the season. Now, as he walked along among the excited fans and heard the cheering for Chip, his feelings were confirmed.

Williams knew all about the feud between Jerry Davis and Henry Rockwell, and he knew that Davis, Waters, and Brasher had ganged up on the veteran coach. He also knew, too, that the three were riding Chip Hilton for some mysterious reason. Williams had concentrated on Brasher during the game. That was how he'd caught the significance of the sideline encounter. He followed the crowd as far as the gym and then started for the locker room.

At the corner, Williams stopped to jot down some notes. As he was writing, Muddy Waters swung around the building and bumped into him, knocking the pen and pad out of Williams's hands. Then Waters made a mistake. He began abusing Williams.

"That's what you get for snooping around," he snarled. "Why don't you stick with your grandstand hero?"

Williams was surprised and unprepared for Waters's aggressive attack, but he kept his head.

"No, Waters, I'm not snooping. But if I were, it wouldn't be too hard to find something for a story. Maybe I'll write that little story about Brasher."

"Lay off Brasher!"

"Like you've laid off Chip Hilton and Henry Rockwell?" Williams replied coolly.

Anger rushed to Waters's sallow face, and then he made his second mistake. He thrust his face close to Williams's and poked the forefinger of his right hand into Pete's chest. "Listen, you Boy Scout," he said angrily, "I'll—"

But that's as far as he got. Williams brushed him aside and turned away. Waters interpreted Williams's retreat as fear and thereupon made his third mistake. He grabbed Pete's left arm and swung him around. Ironically, Pete's outstretched right hand clipped Waters's jaw, and he went down flat on his back. He hadn't even seen the blow coming, and Williams hadn't planned it, but it knocked all the blustering aggressiveness out of Muddy just like air from a punctured balloon. He didn't get up. Waters lay there, frozen by the sudden contact and afraid to move. Williams grinned, picking up his pad and pen before continuing on his way. As Waters struggled to his feet, he heard a snicker. He glanced toward the steps and his face crimsoned. A small, thin man was standing beside the gate, his face in a full grin.

"Bit off more'n you could chew? Aren't you the reporter from the *Times*? Thought you were! Known

A PASS AND A PRAYER

Williams for a long time. Good man! Say, why doesn't your paper write good sports like the *Post* does?"

Waters hurried away. Mark Hanks was a stranger to him, but he knew the encounter would spread all over town before midnight. Muddy was angry, embarrassed, and afraid as he tried to figure out some way to get even with Pete Williams. He'd disliked the popular writer since arriving in Valley Falls. Now he was filled with bitter vindictiveness toward the man who had defended Henry Rockwell and Chip Hilton.

Then he recalled the pathetic spectacle Tom Brasher had made of himself that afternoon. That memory didn't lessen his worries. Brasher's hotheaded foolishness had come close to ruining everything. Davis's plan probably would have been completely upset if the Big Reds hadn't won the game. It didn't look as if he'd be able to deride Hilton in his column this time. The kid had single-handedly pulled the game out of the fire.

It's too bad Waters didn't write his story right then, but he dropped in at his favorite restaurant where Davis and Brasher found him.

"What's wrong with you?" Davis asked, studying Muddy's swollen jaw. "Bad tooth?"

"No, had a fight! Pete Williams."

"Williams? That squirt? What did you do to him? What happened?"

"Oh, he got sanctimonious, and I slapped him around."

Davis was delighted. "Good! Good for you!" Then Jerry's face sunk. "Tom had a fight too. Could be serious. Cracked Hilton in the mouth!"

Waters nearly dropped his coffee cup. He turned to Brasher. "Oh, no, Tom, no! How could you be such a fool? Now you've ruined everything. You can't hit a kid! They'll run you out of town!"

Brasher shook his head angrily. "Ain't nobody runnin' me anywhere. The little jerk jumped me, and I hit him, that's all!"

"But why?" Waters persisted. "I thought everything was all right when I left you at the locker room. When did it happen?"

Brasher had a good imagination, and the story he told seemed plausible. He'd met Hilton in the hall and asked him why he hadn't followed orders. Hilton had become abusive and attacked him. Brasher had merely protected himself. In the scuffle, he had slapped Hilton in the mouth.

The story was believable, but Waters was still worried. "Anyone see it?" he asked.

Brasher shook his head. "No, not a soul."

"You think he'll talk?"

Brasher shrugged his shoulders. "I dunno. I dropped him from the squad. He'll have to talk about that."

"Hilton's pretty reserved," Davis said.

There was a long silence. Davis and Brasher looked to Waters for leadership.

"I'll *have* to break the story," he said worriedly, "have to beat Hilton to the punch. If Williams gets hold of this, he'll play it to the limit. We've got to act quickly. Tom, see Zimmerman right away and report Hilton! Make it strong. Say he jumped you without warning, from behind or something. I'll write the story the same way. You better get goin' now. We'll meet at Jerry's around eleven o'clock."

Tom Brasher knew he'd made a big mistake, but he wasn't particularly worried. He knew Waters and Davis were behind him, and he had Mayor Condon's full support. He assumed an injured demeanor and carefully rehearsed his story as he drove to Carl Zimmerman's house.

As soon as Brasher was out of hearing, Waters boiled over. "The crazy fool!" he growled. "Why'd we get ourselves tied up with such a liability? He's probably ruined the whole plan. We'll have to hustle if we're going to get away with this. We're going to need the help of your friend, the mayor. While I'm writing the story, contact the mayor and get him to make Zimmerman expel the kid. When a kid gets expelled, everyone believes the worst. That's the one thing we've got to engineer: Chip Hilton's expulsion from school for attacking a member of the faculty. Let's get busy! See you at eleven!"

It seemed every football fan in town was looking for Chip Hilton that evening. Everyone was talking about him, and all evening at the Sugar Bowl, Petey Jackson was besieged with questions:

"Where is he?"

"Did he get hurt?"

"Think he's home?"

Mary Hilton was busy too. Her phone rang continuously.

"No, Chip didn't get hurt."

"He's out of town for the weekend."

"He'll be back tomorrow night."

Meanwhile, Henry Rockwell had suffered one of the most critical days since he'd been ill. His blood pressure and temperature had risen so rapidly that Doc Jones confined him to bed and stopped all visitors.

"He'll be all right, Louise," Jones whispered. "It's just the Brasher thing and the excitement of the game. He'll be all right by Monday."

Valley Falls fans were still talking about the game on Sunday, and everyone was eager to get copies of the *Post* and the *Times*. Muddy Waters's column created a sensation.

FALSE HEROES

TIMES AND SPORTS
By Muddy Waters

Star of Hampton Game Dropped Again

Following the Hampton-Valley Falls game, William "Chip" Hilton, captain of the Big Reds football team, was again dropped from the squad by Coach Tom Brasher for insubordination.

Later, it was learned, Hilton attacked Brasher in Brasher's office. Brasher said he had been forced to drop Hilton from the squad on two previous occasions but had permitted the player to return when he promised to control his temper. In yesterday's game with Hampton, Hilton again failed to follow orders and Brasher was again forced to suspend him.

Later, while Brasher was in his office, Hilton entered and, following a wild outburst, attacked and struck the coach several times. Under the circumstances, Brasher said he felt that it was his duty to report the matter to the school authorities for disciplinary action.

Hilton played with exceptional brilliance in yesterday's game following the injury to regular quarterback Tug Rankin, and it is deplorable that the immature athlete is unable to control his temper. Hilton is a natural in all sports, but an athlete who can't control his emotions seldom reaches the heights of stardom for which he is physically qualified.

The Big Reds have won seven straight under the coaching and leadership of Tom Brasher but face their biggest and final test in the quest for the championship of Section Two and the state championship next Saturday when the Big Reds travel to Steeltown.

A PASS AND A PRAYER

Sunday afternoon, Waters, Davis, and Brasher visited Mayor Condon. They left wearing satisfied smiles. Condon had promised to see that Chip Hilton was expelled from school. Furthermore, he assured that Tom Brasher would continue as head coach of football, even if Henry Rockwell returned in time for the Steeltown game.

Speed Morris and Chip Hilton had been traveling all night. They had arrived at their destination and were sitting in the den of Mr. Peters, principal of New Paltz High School, New Paltz, Illinois.

"Yes," Peters was saying, as he examined the program picture, "that's John Rankinowitz, all right. He played football for us last year. In fact, he played four years of football here."

That was all Chip wanted to know, and in a few minutes the two travelers were on their way back to Valley Falls, leaving a puzzled high school principal musing over the strange visit. Chip now had the answer, the answer that would permanently put an end to the mystery of Tom Brasher and Tug Rankin. Now to get back to Valley Falls by Monday.

"Let's move it, Speed," Chip said eagerly.

Speed joked. "What d'ya think I'm doing. This isn't a jet, you know. This is a mean 289 with a three speed."

About that time, Henry Rockwell was checking out of Valley Falls Hospital, and early Monday morning he was in his office at school. Everything was in confusion. Brasher had cleaned out the desk and piled Rockwell's papers in a corner. The Rock was weak but determined to get this situation straightened out, now!

He picked up the phone and soon located Chet Stewart. Stewart was overjoyed and rushed to the office at once. "Hey, Rock," he panted, "it's great to see you. Boy, am I glad you're back!"

Stewart respected Rockwell almost as a father. Chet wouldn't upset Rock by talking about Brasher. He wanted to take care of Tom Brasher personally.

Rockwell got little information from Stewart and headed for Zimmerman's office. At that moment, Mayor Condon was phoning the harassed principal.

"Zimmerman, I understand Rockwell is out of the hospital. If he reports to school, you advise him Brasher will finish out the season. The board expects to release information today that Rockwell is being retired at the end of the year, and Tom Brasher will assume the head coaching responsibilities for football, basketball, and baseball."

Zimmerman was almost speechless. "But, but—"

"No buts! You send him home. He'll be retired as of June 1, but we're going to give him a leave of absence for the rest of the year."

Zimmerman cradled the receiver and shook his head with foreboding. This meant trouble . . . real trouble.

Seconds later, Rockwell was in the office, and Zimmerman was repeating the mayor's words.

"You mean I'm out?"

"Not out, Rock, just retired."

"I don't want to be retired, and I'm not quitting!"

"But, Rock, you're sick. You know you're sick."

"I'm not sick! I'm well! Now you get this! No one moves in on me like that—no one! I'm taking charge! Right now!"

Henry Rockwell was not a profane man, but the language he used to tell Zimmerman what he thought of Condon, Brasher, the school board, the politicians, and eventually Zimmerman himself was extremely forceful, and the mild-mannered principal's ears burned every time he remembered the verbal barrage.

Rockwell was in a furious mood when he returned to his office. The longer he waited for Tom Brasher, the more irate he became. Right after lunch, weak as he was, he found his warm-up and prepared for practice. He was going out and taking charge of his team.

Just as Rockwell finished dressing, Tom Brasher entered the room. He paused in the doorway, clearly surprised. "What are you doing here, Coach? I thought you were in the hospital."

"No, I'm not in the hospital. It's a good thing I got out of there when I did! What's been going on here?"

"Why, nothing unusual, Coach. You probably know I was placed in charge of the team, and I guess you've been advised you've been given a leave of absence for the rest of the year."

"Yes, someone tried to pass that absurdity on to me, but I won't take it. If anyone moves, it will be you," Rockwell said coldly. "I know exactly what you've been up to while I was away. It isn't going to work."

Downstairs, the Big Reds were dressing silently and sullenly. The dead silence in the locker room was the reason they heard the commotion from the office. Chet Stewart bounded up the stairs and burst into the office, with the squad right on his heels.

Brasher had Rockwell pinned in a corner and was punching him savagely. The Rock didn't have a chance in his weakened condition and was unable to withstand the blows of the burly opponent. A second after the door opened, Brasher hit Rockwell savagely, and the pale-faced coach slumped to the floor.

Chet rushed Brasher, but the acting coach was insane with rage and met Chet flush on the jaw with a hard right. Stewart's head hit the desk with a sickening thud. Satisfied, Brasher moved back to Rockwell.

The players stood frozen in shock. A single figure erupted through the door. Brasher was berserk and directed his rage and jarring punches toward Biggie. But they were nothing to the jarring Biggie Cohen gave Tom Brasher. Biggie drove through Brasher's flailing arms as if the blows were drops of water and grasped the raging coach around the body, lifted him from the floor, and heaved him into the wall. Brasher, stunned and afraid, appealed to the only person in the crowd he knew would come to his defense.

"Tug! Tug! Help me out! Help! You owe me!" he cried pathetically.

But Brasher was wrong. He had no friends in that crowd, not even Tug Rankin. Tug turned around and walked out of the office, and Tom Brasher pleaded with Biggie Cohen. "Stop! Please! I've had enough!"

Everybody has one or more sports heroes, and one of Tug Rankin's heroes had been Tom Brasher. He'd never seen the coach the boys called the Rock, but he knew that he was old and had been a very sick man. He'd been horrified at the sight of Brasher beating Rockwell. Right there, a crumbling false hero tumbled from a pedestal.

Now he knew Brasher for the vicious man he was, a man who used deception and intimidation to further his ambitions and who was cowardly enough to attack one man half his size and another twice his age. Tug's first impulse had been to rush to Brasher's side. It was hard to forget that this man was his father's friend and had given the Rankin family new hope in Valley Falls, but then his disgust overwhelmed all thoughts of loyalty, and his friendship for Tom Brasher forever vanished.

A PASS AND A PRAYER

Principal Zimmerman and several teachers had heard the disturbance too and ran to Rockwell's office, pushing the Big Reds players aside. They found Biggie's viselike arms encircling Rock's attacker. Zimmerman and Rockwell, who had recovered somewhat, finally disengaged Biggie's arms from around the cowering coach. Zimmerman ordered them all into his office.

Zimmerman called Mayor Condon immediately and asked him to come right over. "It's a riot!" the shaky principal said brokenly. "A riot!"

Stewart then called Doc Jones. Mayor Condon and Doc Jones arrived together a few minutes later.

Condon's first glance was at Brasher. The man was a sorry sight. Several teeth were loosened, his mouth was bleeding, and he had a black eye and a bloody nose. Condon turned to Zimmerman.

"What is this? What kind of school are you running?" Condon demanded. Then he saw Rockwell. "You," he said sarcastically. "You're hardly out of the hospital, and this is what happens. Consider yourself suspended as of now! The board retired you this morning. Now I'm firing you!"

He turned to Stewart. "And you, you call yourself a coach!" he said angrily, shaking a long finger under Chet's nose. "You're fired too! You've drawn your last check!"

CHAPTER 22

Undefeated, Untied, Uncrowned

SPEED AND CHIP returned to Valley Falls late Monday night. They headed for the Sugar Bowl first and found Petey and Soapy closing up. Soapy was bursting with the news of the big melee, and his graphic account held Chip and Speed spellbound.

"And Zimmerman expelled Biggie, and there's a big meeting scheduled for tomorrow morning, and everyone in town's talkin' about it, and the Rock's back in the hospital, and Chet's in there with a concussion, and this place has been hoppin' all evening, and Brasher's a mess! The guy looks like he's been run through a meat grinder! Wait until you see him!"

"Yeah," Petey added, "and the big jerk said you attacked him after the game and Waters wrote it up in the paper. Did you? What happened?"

Chip was dumfounded. "Attacked him! I never touched him! He hit—Well, never mind. I'll bet my mom's upset about it. I'm going home!"

A PASS AND A PRAYER

Mary Hilton was upset and had been since reading Waters's story. Having Chip home, safe and sound, relieved her anxiety, and she listened eagerly to his story. When he finished, her gray eyes were snapping. "I'm glad you made the trip, Chip. He's an evil man. Now let's call it a day—and what a day."

Chip was in Zimmerman's office the next morning at eight o'clock. The events he told the agitated principal a few minutes later remained forever in the bewildered administrator's memory. But he had sufficient presence of mind to call the mayor and to send for Tom Brasher.

"Now what?" Condon demanded, slamming the door. "Now what's wrong over here?"

Zimmerman was speechless. This situation was too much for him to fathom. He gestured weakly toward Chip. "William, here, has some information that's extremely important."

Condon transferred his glare to Chip. "Well," he growled, "what is it? Speak up!"

Chip had risen to his feet when Condon entered the office, and he remained standing when Valley Falls's chief executive dropped into a chair beside Zimmerman's desk. "Mr. Mayor," he began, "I understand Coach Rockwell and Chet Stewart have been forced to resign."

Condon feigned shock and acted completely flabbergasted. He stood abruptly, looking from Zimmerman to Chip in astonishment. "What is this?" he demanded angrily. "What in the world is this student talking about, Zimmerman? This is the most brazen thing I ever heard. Do the students run this office? Why—"

"Just a second, Mayor," Zimmerman said nervously, walking to the door of the next office. "Tom Brasher is here, and I think he should hear what Chip has to say. Brasher!"

Chip moved back beside the window, and a moment later Brasher entered the room. Chip's eyes widened in surprise. Brasher was a sight. Soapy hadn't exaggerated.

"Well, Hilton!" Condon said impatiently.

Chip looked directly at Tom Brasher. "I think Coach Brasher will understand what I'm getting at, Mayor," Chip replied carefully. "I've just returned from New Paltz, Illinois, where I had a conversation with Mr. Peters, the principal of the high school."

"So what!" Condon looked at Brasher questioningly. "Do you know what he's trying to get at, Tom?"

Brasher was sweating now. Little beads of perspiration formed on his brow, and he wiped them away with a shaking hand. He looked at Condon and cleared his throat while he tried to collect his thoughts. Hilton knew everything. He was ready to reveal it too. Even the look on his face said he was ready.

"I'm . . . I'm not sure, Mayor—er—that is, I think maybe I do."

"Maybe Coach Brasher would rather speak to me privately," Chip suggested.

Brasher nodded eagerly. "Yes, I would. Is it all right, Mayor?"

Condon now was bewildered too. He sighed resignedly and nodded his head. Brasher followed Chip into the outer office.

Chip plunged right in. "I've talked to Mr. Peters, and I know all about Tug Rankin. Furthermore, I'm going to tell the mayor everything I know about you and Tug Rankinowitz, unless you apologize to Coach Rockwell and Chet Stewart and see they're reinstated in their jobs."

Brasher was panic-stricken. He sank down in a chair, his knees shaking. Biggie Cohen had broken his pride and left him only a shadow of his former arrogant, truculent self. He looked like a trapped rat. He seemed to know he couldn't rely on Davis and Waters now, and his mind raced, wildly seeking an escape.

Then he grasped at a thought. "Look, Hilton, you win! You've got all the cards. I'll go along on any kind of a deal you want. But you just can't reveal things about Tug Rankin. Think what it'll mean to the kid and his family. They'll throw him out of school, and his old man will lose his job.

"I know when I've lost. You win and I'll apologize. But look, kid, John Rankin had nothing to do with any part of this. He doesn't know what it's all about, doesn't dream Tug isn't eligible. It's all my fault."

"All right," Chip said firmly, "it's all right with me, except Tug will have to drop out of football. He's ineligible, and you knew it all the time. He played four years at New Paltz, and he played in the East-West game last year, and you were one of the coaches. The whole thing stinks."

"What am I gonna tell the mayor?" Brasher mumbled, rubbing his head nervously.

"That's your problem," Chip said coolly. "You should have thought about that before you brought Tug to Valley Falls."

"All right, Chip, I know now it was wrong. Stick here a minute with me, will you? I'm all mixed up."

Brasher was mixed up because he never once thought of the right thing to do, never once considered telling the truth and facing the consequences. He wasn't that kind of man. He didn't have that kind of courage. He was looking for an easier way out. Then he found the answer, the answer expected from a man of his character: a way to shift the blame to somebody else. Condon was in on this just as much as he was. Hadn't Condon brought Tug here and given his old man a job and forced Zimmerman to let the kid play when he wasn't eligible? If the truth got out, the *Post* never would let it die out. Why, the *Post* would run Condon right out of town!

"All right, Chip. I'll talk to the mayor, and everything will be just the way you want it. Rockwell and Stewart will be reinstated, and Tug will drop out of football. All right?"

Brasher watched Chip intently, and when he saw the senior was still waiting for him to continue, he added, "Oh, yes, I'll apologize too."

Then Chip nodded, turned away, and sat down, and Brasher went into the other office. Zimmerman joined Chip a little later, leaving Brasher closeted with Condon. Half an hour later, Brasher emerged, passing through the office without looking either to the left or the right, and then Zimmerman went inside and closed the door.

Chip waited uncertainly. Occasionally he could hear Mayor Condon's loud voice, but the words were indistinct, and Chip wasn't interested anyway. All he wanted was the reinstatement of Chet and the Rock. He didn't even look up when a little later Condon stomped past him, slamming the door behind him. But his heart jumped joyfully when he heard Zimmerman call his name and saw the smile on the principal's face.

"Everything's fine, Chip. The mayor has reinstated the coach and Chet. From the way he talked, I think Brasher is on his way out. Good riddance! Now sit down and tell me the whole story. You don't need to worry about it going any further, and you can bet your life the mayor and Brasher aren't going to talk. Personally, I want to apologize to you right now for my part in this disgraceful affair.

A PASS AND A PRAYER

"You know, Chip, I, too, thought there was something wrong when Brasher was so set upon entering Rankin in school. I put in a protest. But the student's record was clear, except he'd dropped out of school in his senior year. I never dreamed he'd played four years of football."

Chip then told Zimmerman about his hunch that Brasher knew Rankin before Tug came to Valley Falls and that he'd heard someone refer to Tug as Rankinowitz in Delford.

"But it was the East-West game program that really gave me the answer, Mr. Zimmerman," Chip explained. "Even then, I was going to let the thing work itself out, but when Coach Brasher slugged me, well, I guess I just couldn't stand it any longer."

"You made the right decision, Chip. Your actions saved Rockwell and Stewart from being out of jobs. Don't worry about Biggie Cohen. He was justified in doing exactly as he did. Did a pretty good job too."

Before he left, Chip asked the principal if Tug Rankin would be allowed to stay in school and graduate. Zimmerman made no promises but assured Chip he'd try to help Tug Rankin in every way possible.

Mayor Condon had never been so humiliated in his life. He drove directly to his office and gave orders not to be disturbed. Then he began to sweat it out. His vanity was hurt, and he worried the *Post* might uncover the story. "Waters and Davis got me into this," he fumed. Then he began to think about Chip Hilton, who he grudgingly had to admit handled the situation and Tom Brasher like a champion.

"He's a clever kid," he mused, "far too clever for an inane man like Brasher. I've got to distance myself from Brasher and this mess. He's stupid and dangerous.

Rankin, I can use. He's been invaluable in his job. Besides, Brasher's stirred up enough trouble. If I let Rankin go now, I'd stir up another hornet's nest. Probably get that Hilton kid on my back again, and then I'd be in trouble."

John Rankin was timid, almost shy, in his contacts with other men. He'd never played sports, and he'd been awed by Tug's football prowess. But deep under his gentle conduct was a fervent desire that his son would secure an education, and be better equipped than he was to meet life's responsibilities. The move to Valley Falls had been a great break, perhaps the best he had ever known. But there was no regret in his heart as he listened to his son, nothing but pride that his son was man enough to realize his mistakes and admit them. Tug had already played four years of football, and that wasn't right. He nodded his head sympathetically as Tug continued.

"I just couldn't go to school this morning, Dad, knowing I've been playing under false pretenses and all that, but I've made up my mind. I'm going to see Mr. Zimmerman and tell him the whole story."

"How will all this affect Tom Brasher, Tug?"

"I guess he'll lose his job, Dad. I guess he ought to lose it. I know what I have to do is going to be rough on you, and it means I'll have to leave school. But I've got to do it. I'm wrong, and I intend to face it and take the punishment."

John Rankin placed his arm around his son's shoulders and gripped him tight. His eyes were proud and happy. "I'm glad you're man enough to do this, Tug. You'll never know how glad I am you're big enough to face such a situation."

A PASS AND A PRAYER

Carl Zimmerman knew Tug Rankin only as a transfer student who could play football. He had admired the boy's ability, but he'd been skeptical of his character and spirit of sportsmanship. But his admiration grew as Tug told everything that had happened from the first day Tom Brasher had asked him to come to Valley Falls.

Tug told Zimmerman he'd met Brasher in the previous year's East-West game. He'd been surprised but happy when the coach had asked him to come to Valley Falls and play. He'd reminded Brasher he'd already played four years and wouldn't be eligible, but Brasher had said it was all right; he said age and eligibility didn't matter. Tug's voice faltered when he told how badly his father had needed a job and what it had meant to him. Tug didn't forget to tell about the stadium lesson Chip had given him either. Then he brought out a factor that Zimmerman had overlooked.

"I'm sorry all the victories will have to be forfeited, Mr. Zimmerman. It's going to be awfully tough on the team, especially Chip."

The worried principal had let Rankin tell the story in his own way, never intimating he already knew everything. As he listened, something happened to Carl Zimmerman. He grew up, came of age, and became responsible for his own job. He resolved to make his own decisions and act without help or directive from Mayor Condon.

"I'll take care of the forfeitures right away, Tug," he said kindly. "All the other details too. But I want to set you straight about something important. You're still in good academic standing here, and I'm going to see you remain that way. Naturally, you won't be permitted to play football, but you can forget about any interference with your schooling. Now go home, do some studying, and get back in your classes tomorrow morning. I'm glad you feel the way you do about Chip Hilton, Tug. I guess neither of us has to worry about him! He's playing in the East-West game, you know."

That night, at the Sugar Bowl, Chip received a call from Principal Zimmerman. "Chip, Brasher has resigned from Valley Falls effective immediately. I still say he's fortunate that there will be no charges against him, but other action has been taken. The vice principal, Ms. Pearce, and I met with Brasher this afternoon. That's when he resigned and also agreed to and signed the letter Ms. Pearce and I drafted to the State Department of Education requesting his teaching license be terminated. He's through in teaching and coaching, Chip.

"By the way," he added, chuckling gently, "the Rock and Chet Stewart won't be able to attend the game against Steeltown, and I'm appointing you as student-coach. You'll be the captain, the quarterback, and the coach of the team! I'll travel with the team and be on the sidelines with you as the administrator."

The rest of that week was the strangest in the history of Valley Falls High School football. Because Chip Hilton, the Big Reds captain and quarterback, served as student-coach of the team, and he was still in charge when the bus rolled out of town for the trip to Steeltown. Despite the knowledge the Steelers had backed into the championship of Section Two due to the forfeiture of all the games Tug Rankin had played in, every player on the squad was determined to prove Valley Falls High was the best team and would emerge the only undefeated team in the state.

Coach Chip Hilton had a good assistant. A person by the name of Tug Rankin. Tug ran the bench and was treated as though he'd been a regular of the Hilton A. C. all of his life instead of its newest member.

Knowing Chip Hilton, you would have expected the Big Reds to show their wide-open passing game that afternoon. But the game developed into a kicking duel. Passing was impossible because it had rained all morning and during every minute of the game. Near the end of the game, Chip Hilton, standing almost ankle-deep in mud, booted a field goal to give the Big Reds a 3-0 victory and an undefeated season. Knowing Chip Hilton and the rest of the Big Reds, you wouldn't have been surprised to learn the happy team presented Tug Rankin with the game ball and hoisted him up on the players' shoulders. The Big Reds were like that.

• • •

A MYSTERIOUS STRANGER arrives in Valley Falls representing himself as a former classmate of Chip Hilton's father, when Big Chip was starring at State University. As everybody knows, Valley Falls is a hot basketball town, but when word gets around that the stranger is a great shot, he soon has the place hoop crazy. When three-point fever spreads to the Big Red team and dissension threatens team unity, Coach Rockwell and Chip Hilton find themselves in trouble.

Be sure to read *Hoop Crazy,* the next exciting story in Coach Clair Bee's Chip Hilton Sports series.

Afterword

THE CHIP HILTON SERIES is back—what exciting news for all of us who grew up following Chip's adventures! For everyone who read from *Touchdown Pass* to *Hungry Hurler,* this is truly great. For me it has special meaning. As a young coach out of Penn State, my first coaching and teaching job was at New York Military Academy and my boss was Clair Bee. Coach Bee, as we all called him, was the athletic director at NYMA and hired me to be with him as assistant football and head basketball coach, as well as teach all grades and intramurals and be a "father" to the young cadets.

Besides coaching, Coach Bee taught me many, many things about teaching and working with players. He was truly a master of technique, strategy, and psychology. He had it—and I was so fortunate to have Coach Bee as my mentor. My years with Coach Bee also included summer camps at Kutchers Country Club in the Catskills. Kids and coaches from all over the country wanted to be with

Coach Bee. What he instilled in all of us was knowledge, preparation, and discipline that were needed to put a winning team on the field. I carried these lessons with me to the NFL as a coach and now as a general manager.

I'm proud to say that I was blessed to have the opportunity to work beside a great person and a great coach. Chip Hilton books went with me. The book I treasured the most was his *Touchdown Pass* that he signed to our son, Chip, when he was born. I'm proud to say that Chip has lived up to his namesake, Chip Hilton, and I do believe that Coach Bee would smile and be equally as proud.

JOHN E. BEAKE
General Manager, Denver Broncos Football Club

more great releases from the

Chip Hilton Sports Series

by Coach Clair Bee

The sports-loving boy, born out of the imagination of Clair Bee, is back! Clair Bee first began writing the Chip Hilton Series in 1948. During the next twenty years, over two million copies of the series were sold. Written in the tradition of the *Hardy Boys* mysteries, each book in this 23-volume series is a positive–themed tale of human relationships, good sportsmanship, and positive influences — things especially crucial to young boys in the '90s. Through these larger-than-life fictional characters, countless young people have been exposed to stories that helped shape their lives.

WELCOME BACK, CHIP HILTON!

TOUCHDOWN PASS
#1
0-8054-1686-2

CHAMPIONSHIP BALL
#2
0-8054-1815-6

available at fine bookstores everywhere